PARLAY

PARLAY

JOEY TRUMAN

Whisk(e)y Tit

NYC & Vermont

Published in the United States by Whisk(e)y Tit: www.whiskeytit.com. If you wish to use or reproduce all or part of this book for any means, please let the author and publisher know. You're pretty much required to, legally.

ISBN 978-0-9996215-4-7

Cover art by George Truman and Jack Warren. Cover design by Murphey Wilki Edited by Tina Satter.

First Whisk(e)y Tit paperback edition.

To KSS, you are the Runa to my Captain Whitey

From *Postal Child*

Whitey spent the nights walking up and down the streets of Park Slope. In his mind he was delivering mail. He would stop at trash cans on the corner thinking they were pick-up points and take trash out of the cans. Whitey would put these things in his cart. He delivered a banana peel to 331 St. Marks. An empty beer can to 208 Dean. And a styrofoam container to the drain at Fifth Avenue and Bergen.

This went on for three weeks. Whitey woke up hungry and dehydrated next to the Gowanus Canal, splayed out on a comfortable patch of grass.

1

He called him Doctor Sunshine. He had white feathers and a yellow breast. He was a pretty bird. Whitey took him everywhere. He rode on top of his mail cart. His first mate, Whitey would think. Lately he had felt like a pirate. Whitey had. A change had come over him. Whitey didn't know it though. He had been walking down the street minding his own business, but then, out of nowhere, a smell slapped him in the face. His mom. He smelled his mom. A thousand wires got crossed in his brain. He always had trouble processing information, but this smell, his mother floating in the breeze did him in. He spun around looking for her. He couldn't find her. His memory broke open. A repressed shattered dyke. Suddenly he was back at Jonx and Brandy's again. Covered in shit. Hungry and frightened. Then an oblivion. A blackness. An infinite rip in his mortal timeline. Then a light. A shimmering highness, paper white. And blue, and red, and yellow. He woke a new man. A pirate and a savior. A deliverer. A deliverer of the good news, the parcels of peace and goodwill. He was a new man indeed. And he, he and Doctor Sunshine would spread the word. He was sure of this.

In Whitey's mind it was spring. He needed to get his ship together. The winter had been a cold and dark horror. He had been holed up in a small inn on the edge of the great Gowanus Canal. The ice was finally melting. Its ceaseless creaking made his muscles ache. He yearned for the freedom of the open sea. His only companion during those dark and dreary days the winter brought was Doctor Sunshine. They would talk by candlelight about the treasures the open sea would bring. Plotting and scheming. They would sail down to the Bahamas and intercept tobacco ships, spice ships, slave ships. The riches knew no bounds. They only needed crew. Doctor Sunshine was put in charge of getting crew. Whitey made lists, and outfitted the ship. Before long they were ready to sail.

Whitey was standing on the corner of Bergen and Hoyt when Doctor Sunshine showed up with two new crew members. Whitey was digging in a trash can looking for rope. He found a mop head. What luck! The birds landed on the edge of the trash can. Whitey stood erect. The birds saluted him. He saluted back. Doctor Sunshine said:

"Sir, this is Detective Rabbi, and Moiler, they have signed on."

"Great, great. Let's get to work. Untangle this rope."

Whitey put the mop head on the sidewalk and spread it out. The birds went to work. They untangled the strands. Whitey took Doctor Sunshine aside and said:

"These men look like good seafaring men, can you get more?"

"Of course, sir."

"Well, good."

Doctor Sunshine flew away. Whitey poked around in the trash can some more. He was looking for hardtack. He found some soggy saltines, drenched in coffee grounds. He smiled. They were still in their plastic package. He put them in his mail cart. He looked down at Detective Rabbi and Moiler, they were making progress on the mop. They seemed like a good crew. Things were looking shipshape.

2

An hour later Whitey was sitting on the stoop next to the trash can. He had called a break. Detective Rabbi and Moiler were sweating. At least in Whitey's mind. They were sitting on his knees. Whitey was giving them the rundown of the situation:

"Ok, boys, this is gonna be a hard run. Do you know what parlay is?" The pigeons bobbed their heads. "Good, we're gonna fuck them bastards up! Are you two good with the pistol?" The pigeons bobbed their heads. "Good, I am going to grow a mustache, you should too, that way we can light it on fire and shoot faster. Ok, let's get back to work."

Whitey went back to digging in the trash. Detective Rabbi and Moiler went back to unbraiding the mop head. Doctor Sunshine came back, alone. He landed on the mail cart. Whitey looked at him. His face looked dejected. Whitey's shoulders dropped. He knew they must move on. In order to find more crew, they must move on. Whitey picked up the mop head, he stowed it in the mail cart. He told Detective Rabbi and Moiler to come aboard. They flew up and perched themselves on the top of the mail cart. They saluted Whitey. He saluted back. He pushed the mail cart down the block. The next trash can was a bust. It was completely empty. Whitey spied a park down the way. He yelled:

"Land ho!"

Whitey took the birds into the park and found a bench. He was tired and needed some sleep. He took the blankets from the mail cart. The blankets were newspapers. He wedged himself under the park bench. It was dark now. The birds clucked around for a while before coming to bed. He was happy when they did. They were warm and nice. He was asleep before he knew it.

3

The morning light shown through the slats of the park bench. The birds were already awake. Clucking around. Pecking around. Biting the ground for food. Whitey got up and stretched. He yawned and folded the newspaper blankets. He put them in the mail cart. He went over to the drinking fountain. He took a drink. He brushed his teeth with his index finger. He pulled his pants down and washed his genitals and his ass. The morning sun felt nice on his bottom. He stood there for a second drying off. His balls felt heavy and his penis became stiff. Doctor Sunshine flew up and landed on his erect perch. Whitey said:

"Well, good morning, Doctor Sunshine, I trust you slept well?"

"I did, I did, sir. I trust you did too?"

Whitey's penis slowly deflated. Doctor Sunshine held on as the perch disappeared. Doctor Sunshine was at a weird angle when he finally let go. He opened his wings and fluttered to the ground. Whitey pulled up his pants. He was dry enough. His penis hurt from Doctor Sunshine's claws. He was bleeding, but he didn't mind. Pirates don't mind about bloody dicks. That's not what pirates do.

Doctor Sunshine cooed around for a bit while Whitey made sure he had all his things. Detective Rabbi and Moiler had already gone off to recruit more crew. They would meet up later at the port, Whitey decided. He told Doctor Sunshine to come aboard. Doctor Sunshine flew up onto the cart. Whitey whistled a dirge. Then they were off.

4

Call and response. "Yo ho ho and a bottle of rum." Followed by "chirp chirp chirp and a chirper of chirp." They cruised the streets looking for victuals. At one garbage can they found a half-eaten hot-dog and a bottle of urine. Whitey poured the urine out into the gutter. He looked down into the bottle and declared the vessel to be "of poor quality," and threw it back in the trash can. The hot-dog passed muster.

On the next corner the trash can only had newspaper. The newspaper held dog shit. Whitey shook his head. "The quality of blankets these days, right, Doctor Sunshine?" Doctor Sunshine bobbed his head.

There were two long blocks before they got to the canal. They would set up camp and wait for Detective Rabbi and Moiler. Whitey was nervous that it was getting late in the season. He was worried about provisions, but he knew he needed crew. He and Doctor Sunshine sat down, waiting. The sun slowly crept across the early morning sky. Doctor Sunshine got bored and flew off to,"boink some babes." Whitey sat there, listening to the water slowly pass by, bending the grass that was growing on the edge. He licked the ketchup and mustard from the hot-dog he had acquired, careful not to eat the meat, even though he wanted to.

Two hours went by. Whitey fell asleep with boredom. He woke to little bouncing on his stomach. There were three birds hopping around. One was Detective Rabbi and one was Moiler. The other one was unknown to Whitey. Detective Rabbi told Whitey his name:

"This is The Talker, we got the crew! Where is Doctor Sunshine?"

"He went to boink some babes, good to meet you, I'm Captain Whitey, welcome aboard!" Whitey saluted them. They saluted him back. Whitey sat up. The birds jumped to the ground. They bobbed and preened themselves. They took shits. Detective Rabbi pecked at some things. The air smelled like oil and burned garlic. "We still need victuals. You guys know where to get some, I am coming up empty." The Talker said:

"I know this place just down the road, donuts and bagels."

"Show me."

Captain Whitey stood up. The birds hopped on top of his cart. He pushed them towards the place that The Talker knew about. The sun was hot now. The going was slow. Captain Whitey hoped that Doctor Sunshine would be able to find him when he was done boinking the girls. He had a full crew now. He needed victuals and suddenly he realized he needed weapons, but who has weapons? He decided he would think about this later. Now, victuals. Weapons after. Part of him relaxed, but another part of him was on edge. The Talker was a talker. He liked to talk. He made noise. Noise after noise after noise. He talked:

"Where are we going? You know what I think of that, it smells pretty bad, did you ever think about that? What is that smell? I mean, that is a pretty bad smell, what's that smell? Do you like smells? I like smells, how come nobody asks me how I am feeling? What's that over there? What do I look like, a jerk? How come I can smell that and you can't?"

"Jesus, Talker, drop it!" Moiler said.

"Drop what, I am just saying, you ever say something? See something, say something, that's my motto."

"Ugh, you're gonna get punched."

"Punch? I love punch, Hawaiian, blueberry, fruit punch, the combo punch, watermelon." The Talker talked himself into a frenzy. He flew away squawking into the air. Everybody breathed a sigh of relief. Captain Whitey said:

"What the hell was that? He coming back?"

"He always comes back," Moiler said.

"Oh, lord."

They found themselves at the donut and bagel depository. The trash can was full of hardtack. Whitey took a bag from the dumpster. They were ready to set sail. He threw the bag over his shoulder. They walked back to the canal to wait for Doctor Sunshine. The walk was nice and quiet since The Talker was gone. Whitey hoped that Doctor Sunshine was done boinking the girls and would help him find some weapons. A new recruit flew down and landed on the mail cart. A weird bird. He didn't coo like the others. Instead he just made beeping noises. Captain Whitey decided to call him Beeper. Beeper seemed nice and helpful. Detective Rabbi was stoic, and Moiler seemed nice and angry. He had a good crew, Captain Whitey did, the only thing he was missing was a cabin boy.

5

Formation. Captain Whitey watched a formation of pigeons fly an "S" pattern around the top of a building and down into a tree. He noticed a finch. He'd never seen a finch flying with pigeons before. The bird seemed small in respect. Faster. More agile. Captain Whitey was impressed. He turned to Detective Rabbi and said:

"What do you think of that guy? The small guy, the fast one?"

"He's a finch sir."

"Go get him, I want to talk to him."

Detective Rabbi flew up into the tree. A moment later he flew back and landed on the mail cart. The finch landed beside him. Detective Rabbi said:

"Captain Whitey, this is Finch. He's a finch."

"Good to meet you, Finch. I am Captain Whitey. Are you a cabin boy, Finch?"

"I am a cabin boy, Captain Whitey. Are you looking for a cabin boy, Captain Whitey?"

"I am indeed, Finch. We are about to set sail, argh, are you willing?"

"I am willing, argh."

"Well, welcome aboard!"

Captain Whitey had a water bottle filled with water from the drinking fountain. He took the cap off and poured some water into the lid. He put it in front of Detective Rabbi and Finch. They drank from it. Captain Whitey took a drink from the bottle. In his mind he was drinking rum. He said:

"Argh! To the high seas!"

"Aye! Aye!"

The two birds drank deep and hard. The crew was full.

When they got back to the canal they settled down and made camp. Detective Rabbi and Finch got drunk and passed out on the grass. Doctor Sunshine came back covered in smooches. Moiler and Beeper made a tiny fire using little twigs they found. They started roasting worms. The Talker was nowhere to be seen, Whitey was glad of this. That guy talks too much, he thought as he made a bed for himself. After I make my daily log I will talk to Doctor Sunshine, we got work to do, can't have him gallivanting like that.

After setting up camp Captain Whitey sat down with his thoughts. He picked up a twig and a leaf from the ground and started writing:

Day one, already missing home. Camp is set up nice, we got enough victuals for the trip. Cabin Boy! Finch seems good. Doctor Sunshine is a bit of a wild cat, but you can't breed the beast out of the animal. Moiler and Detective Rabbi are capable but seem to like the rum a little much, and The Talker is a bit of noisy Nelly, but I think he will do. All in all, I have a good crew. I have my doubts about Beeper, he seems a little slow, but time will tell. I am hoping to set sail within the fortnight. The weather seems to be holding.

Captain Whitey put his writing in his pocket and called for Doctor Sunshine to come over. Doctor Sunshine hopped over and jumped onto Captain Whitey's knee. He said:

"Captain Whitey?"

"Did you clean your pipes?"

"I did indeed, sir."

"Are you ready to sail?"

"I am indeed, sir."

"Good. You meet our cabin boy, Finch?"

"I did, sir, seems solid, sir."

"Good. Weather seems right, any thoughts? I am thinking we should wait a couple days."

"Weather is nice, but I feel a breeze. Let's wait for the sunset and see."

"Agreed. You have a good time? You are covered in hickeys! Ha!"

"Only the best, sir, them Brooklyn babes are top notch! Hats off!"

"Yes, they are. Come back after dark, let's talk."

"You got it, sir."

Doctor Sunshine hopped down from Captain Whitey's leg and went back to the twig fire with the roasting worms. Captain Whitey looked up at the sky. He lay down, watching the clouds drift from his right side to his left side of vision. A few minutes went by. He fell asleep.

8

The sleep Captain Whitey took was a nap. He woke up refreshed. The smell of the canal blew across one nostril and poked its greasy mariner-y modus right directly into the other nostril Captain Whitey had. He reached his arms into the air and yawned. He felt alive.

All the pigeons were gone, except Doctor Sunshine. He was poking coals from the worm fire and waiting for Captain Whitey to wake up. The tip of his wings were covered in soot. Night was upon them. Doctor Sunshine wasn't brooding, but his demeanor looked dejected. Captain Whitey walked over and sat down. He said:

"You look dejected, mate, a penny for your thoughts."

"I don't know, I don't know. You got a penny, sir?"

"Of course, you need one?"

"I don't know, didn't you offer me one?"

"I mean, I guess, you need a penny?"

"I don't know, you did offer me one."

"Sorry, I know, you're right, I did offer you one, but I don't actually have one, but what are you thinking?

"Now I am thinking about pennies, why did you offer me one if you didn't have it?"

"I don't know, isn't that what people say?"

"I don't know, what do I know about people?"

"I would think you would know enough about people to know that they paid a penny for thoughts."

"That's my point, Captain Whitey, a penny goes a long way."

"But I don't have a penny."

"Well then stop offering it to me."

"But I didn't, not really."

"Yes, you did."

Captain Whitey and Doctor Sunshine sat there looking at the twigs smolder. Their misunderstanding felt like anger, but it wasn't. They were learning to communicate. He needed him, and he needed him. The stinky air drifted through Captain Whitey's nose. Doctor

Sunshine didn't have a nose. He picked at his feathers. His hickeys were starting to bruise. Had he had teeth in his beak, one would have been missing. He smelled like bent metal and oil dust. The night was black. They took a moment and waited. A moment later Captain Whitey said:

"We got a half a hot-dog, I licked the condiments off though, is that a problem?"

"No, sir, only practical, you wrap it up?"

"No, not as yet, that is first business. You see the bag of hardtack? I think tomorrow we need to dry that out, that is, if this rain don't fall, you really think we got a nor'easter brewing?"

"I do, sir. We should maybe tarpaulin the tack and expect for the worst. I sent Finch out to get more rope so we could dangle the tack."

"Good, good. Yes, yes."

"The wind is picking up."

"I feel that too, we need the men now, how do we call?"

"I'll send Finch, here he is now."

Finch showed up with a beak full of hair that he found in the gutter. Doctor Sunshine told him to go get the crew. A storm was brewing. Finch flew off. Captain Whitey and Doctor Sunshine tied hairs onto bagels and donuts. Then they attached them to the bottom of the mail cart. The wind increased. Finch came back with all the birds except The Talker. He was still missing. They all battened down the hatches. Some of them had hickeys. They were drunk, but worked hard.

The bagels and donuts were flapping in the breeze. The mail cart was swaying but seemed steady. The bagels and donuts turned and flapped, holding strong. All the birds were battening down the hatches. Suddenly a splash of water came up onto the shore. It was greasy. The birds flew for cover. Captain Whitey ditched into a low spot on the ground. He only got kind of wet. The smell from the canal got worse and Captain Whitey was scared for a moment. His courage returned. He ran to the mail cart and made sure it stood upright. The wind blew on his restive skin. He would die for this storm. He would die for the birds. He would die, if that would mean they would make it through the night.

The storm continued. Around three in the morning it stopped. Captain Whitey was broken and exhausted. The storm had left them. He made sure all the crew was alive. They were. The hardtack was soaked, and the half hot-dog was gone. All that Captain Whitey could do as the sun came up in the peaceful, easy eastern morning was to shake his head in disappointment.

9

Captain Whitey watched the sun rise. When the sun was truly upon him he took a nap. When he woke up he was hot and sweaty. The birds were gone. The camp was a mess. He cleaned up the best he could, but everything was so water-soaked that he gave up. He was back to zero. He put his cap on, he couldn't remember if he had had a cap before. The storm had broken his memory. He tried to think for a minute, but it didn't help. He looked down at his dirty and greasy postal outfit and shrugged. I must be a postman, he thought. He stood up and walked over to his mail cart. He lifted the flap on one side. The contents were dry. He lifted the flap on the other side. The results were the same. He shrugged. He looked around for a clock, or something that would tell him the time. He found nothing. I must be running late, he thought to himself. He walked down to the canal and pissed. The canal smelled like baby diarrhea. He went back to the mail cart and said out loud, "Back to work."

Whitey pushed the cart with a confusion he couldn't suss out. He felt like he should be doing something, but he didn't know what that something was. He found himself casually digging through a trash can ten blocks from the canal looking for the VIN number on a banana peel when The Talker showed back up. The Talker landed on the mail cart and said:

"Captain, Captain, you know what I mean by that? What are you doing? I mean, what's with the banana? I mean, where's the crew? Crew is a pretty good word, 'C'-roo, like kangaroo, what do you know about kangaroos? I like kangaroos, I mean, what's with the banana, you like bananas? I mean, come on, give me a break, you know what I mean?"

The Talker flew away. This confused Whitey. That was a weird bird, he thought, and where the hell is the VIN number on this goddamn banana peel? Whitey stamped it "undeliverable," by kissing the banana peel and throwing it back in the trash can. He moved down the block.

The next three trash cans held nothing of interest. The fourth one did. It was a broken blue flip-flop with a hank of bacon grease snagged on the tip. To Whitey's eyes it meant "Priority." He delivered it as fast as he could to the mailbox that was underneath a potted plant that was on the stoop of 344 Union. He rang the bell twice and when nobody answered he walked on.

He was two houses down when someone came out. It was a woman. She yelled:

"Hey! What the hell?!" She was waving the flip-flop at him.

"You're welcome, ma'am!" Whitey held up his arm, waving. He was happy he had done his job.

At the end of the block The Talker came back. Whitey was taking a break. The priority delivery had really taken it out of him. He was sitting on a standpipe, feeling proud of himself. The idea of ice cream crossed his mind. The Talker landed on the ground at Whitey's feet. He said:

"I mean it, you know what I mean? But seriously, where is the crew? I mean, you know what I meant by that? I went back to the camp, see, and listen, but where is the crew?"

"What the hell are you talking about? Leave me alone, I'm on a break."

"What are you talking about? I mean, where are the guys?"

"Get lost." Whitey kicked at The Talker and he flew away. He wasn't gone for long. He sat on top of a fence for a second and then flew right back. He stood there bobbing on the sidewalk next to Whitey's feet. He said:

"Tell me where the guys are, tell me where the guys are."

"What are you talking about?"

"The guys, the crew, where are the guys, the crew?"

"Leave me alone, which guys? What crew?"

"Doctor Sunshine, Moiler, Detective Rabbi, Beeper, Finch, you know what I mean? The crew."

"I don't know what you mean, leave me alone, I am on a break, I just had an intense delivery, I'm tired."

"You know what I think of that? It stinks. What do you mean, you don't know what I mean? You're stupid. You know how I can tell you are stupid? It's because you are a jerk. That's how. You'll see, you want to know how you'll see? You'll see!" The Talker flew away.

Whitey sat on the standpipe resting his bones. He folded his arms. He knew who would see about whom and for what! He started to remember about his plans to take a pirate ship onto the high seas. He cursed that stupid bird for being right. He had business to attend to. He stood up and pushed his mail cart back towards the canal.

10

The birds were waiting for him when he got back to the canal. They were standing in formation. Formation meant they were all bobbing around and shitting on things and pecking at the ground. Captain Whitey had a moment of proudness. He parked the mail cart to the side and gave a speech:

"Men, men, my men, as God as my witness, my men!"

The birds all shit in unison out of respect. In Captain Whitey's mind they saluted him with their wings. Captain Whitey continued his speech:

"Our hardtack is gone, and one of you fuckers ate the half hot-dog we were saving for the voyage, but not all is lost, we may be hungry, we may be lonely, we may in fact be poorly prepared, but we will, as God as my witness, my men, persevere!"

The birds clapped their wing tips together. They yelled, "Huzzah!" Captain Whitey bowed. He was so proud of himself he couldn't believe it. He dismissed his men and asked Doctor Sunshine for a private consultation.

Doctor Sunshine came over. The other birds made themselves busy setting up camp. Captain Whitey sat down so as to be closer to Doctor Sunshine. Doctor Sunshine said:

"Sock it to me, Cappy."

"Drop the formalities, man, you know what I did today?"

"Sure thing, sir, of course, I talked to The Talker."

"I'm worried I might be losing it, I just need to know I got somebody in my corner if the shit hits the fan, you know what I mean by the fan?"

"No, sir, I don't know what a fan is."

"Oh, of course, yeah, of course you don't, it's this round thing that makes air, with blades and such."

"Shit, sir, sounds scary!"

"Oh no! It's a good thing."

"Yeah, but shit hits it, and it has blades, and…"

"Forget the fan, I just need you to take over for me if my brain stops working, is all."

"Ok, sir. And how will I know that, sir?"

"I don't know, but I think you will. Doctor Sunshine, you are the only one I trust."

"I know that, sir."

"Ok, good. Tomorrow we parlay, you reckon?"

"Yes, sir, I reckon, sir."

"Ok, good. Now get some sleep, I need some too."

Doctor Sunshine joined the men making camp. He barked a couple orders in a way that looked like he was pecking the ground and cooing. Captain Whitey took some newspapers from the mail cart and made himself a bed. He was either in for a night of wonderful rest, or a night of anxiety and bleakness. It was still early though, so he just lay down and watched planes fly over. He realized he hadn't eaten anything in a while. He thought he should do that soon. He drifted off to sleep.

11

When Captain Whitey woke up The Talker was standing on his forehead. The cleats of his toes were digging into his skin. He brushed him aside and checked his lips for fodder and drippings. Captain Whitey knew that birds were worse than cockroaches sometimes. They left a trail. When the back of his hand came away clean he sat up. He asked The Talker:

"What's up?"

"Oh, nothing, you know what I mean? I mean, what are you doing? Sleeping?"

"I guess so, what's up?"

"I don't know, I mean, why did you wake up? Are you done being tired? I mean, did you sleep enough? If I sleep too much I get a headache, do you have a headache? Did you sleep too much? Why don't you answer my questions? Did you know I was asking you a question? I didn't sleep too much, in fact I slept the right amount, you know what I mean? I mean, what the hell?"

"Talker! What's up? Why did you wake me up?"

"Oh, that's how it is, if it's gonna be that way, maybe I shouldn't tell you, you know what I mean? Like because you don't want to have a conversation with me, maybe I should not tell you the information I came over to wake you up about, you know, the information I was going to tell you? You know? I mean, do you even know? What I mean, I mean?"

"I am sorry Talker, what is it you mean? Please tell me."

"Yeah, ok, I mean, if you mean it, I mean, you look tired, did you just wake up? How come you have claw marks on your forehead? What I mean to say is, Moiler found some more victuals, he wants to talk to you."

"Thanks, Talker, can you send him over?"

"Sure thing, Captain Whitey, I tried to send him over in the first place, but he thought I should do it, you know what I mean? I don't know why though, you know what I meant by that? I mean, why would he have me come talk to you? You know what I mean? What's the point, I mean? You know what I meant?"

Captain Whitey looked over at Moiler. He was laughing. Captain Whitey shook his head. He told The Talker to get lost. He waved Moiler over. Moiler came over. He sat down and packed his pipe. He asked Captain Whitey for a match. Captain Whitey lit his pipe. Then Captain Whitey said:

"You swarthy cunt."

"What? It's your crew, who am I to have some fun?" Moiler smiled. He sucked on his pipe stem. In Whitey's mind he had an earring. He blew smoke out his nose holes.

"Yeah, well, meet your new bunkmate, hope it was worth it."

"Fucking hell. Don't do that to me."

"We'll see, what's your information? Your bunker says you have a lead on some tack?"

"Very much, sir, I spotted some victuals on Union, if we leave now, we might just have a chance to parlay."

"Very well, organize the crew, we leave in five, and inform The Talker I have changed his name to Bunker, is that clear?"

"Yes, sir."

"Very well, parlay!"

"Parlay!"

Captain Whitey folded up his newspapers and put them in his mail cart. Moiler went and told the crew to get ready to parlay. He also told The Talker his new name was Bunker. The Talker, now Bunker, bobbed his head in agreement. Two minutes went by. Then Captain Whitey shouted:

"Parlay!"

He pushed the mail cart towards Union Street. All the birds, including Finch, the cabin boy, rode on his shoulders. In Whitey's mind they had guns and mustaches and eye patches and peg legs and hooked wings and were smoking pipes and cigars and had black grease smeared on their faces. They looked mean. Smoke was billowing from all the places smoke billows from. They stank terrible. And were ready to rape and pillage and plunder.

In reality, they were just a guy pushing a mail cart down the street and some pigeons and a finch on his shoulders. The back of his jacket covered in bird shit. A smile on his face. Walking toward Union Street to get some bread from a dumpster.

12

When Captain Whitey spotted the dumpster he yelled:

"Port side mates! We got a live one brewing!"

Beeper and Bunker hauled ass. They took the port side. Meaning they hopped onto the front of the mail cart. Bobbing and cooing. Captain Whitey yelled:

"Man the gunners, mates! We gotta wrench those cunts!"

Detective Rabbi and Moiler hauled ass. They took the starboard side. Meaning they hopped on the handle of the mail cart. Bobbing and cooing. Captain Whitey yelled:

"All hands on deck!"

Doctor Sunshine and Finch hauled ass. Finch flew up to the crow's nest. Which meant the top of Captain Whitey's hat. Doctor Sunshine jumped onto Captain Whitey's arm. He bobbed and cooed.

The ship was ready to attack. Captain Whitey yelled:

"Finch!"

"Yes, sir?"

"Port clear?"

"Clear port, sir!"

"Beeper, Bunker? Port side clear?"

"Clear, Captain!" they said in unison.

"Finch!"

"Sir?"

"Starboard?"

"Clear, starboard!"

"Detective Rabbi, Moiler?"

"Starboard, clear!" they said in unison.

"Hope you settled your affairs, boys, because you are about to die, attack!"

Captain Whitey pushed the mail cart across the street. He wasn't running. In fact, he had to wait for a car to pass. When the car passed, he crossed the street. There were people milling around. Some had bags of groceries. Some were just walking by. In his mind, the birds were attacking everybody in sight. They were running for cover, the people in sight. A cannon was shot. A leg got lost. The air smelled of smoke and blood. There was a grimace on Captain Whitey's face. His eyes were as cold and direct as if he had been sanding a piece of wood. He blew a breath. A cloud of dust erupted into the sky. Captain Whitey could suddenly see the thing they were attacking. He yelled:

"Moiler! Attack! Parlay! Detective Rabbi, burn the ditch! Make orphans of their babies!"

"I'm out of ammo!" Beeper yelled.

"Heads down!" Bunker found himself covered in dust.

"Finch! Locate! Finch!"

Captain Whitey pushed on. When he got to the dumpster it was in fact filled with bread. The dumpster was metal. It was blue. The birds were useless as Captain Whitey took a bag out of the dumpster. The people that were milling around felt guilty as they watch him do this. They knew he was not entirely correct and probably needed help. They were happy he got some food though. They would have probably given him money if he had asked them. But they didn't. And he didn't. Captain Whitey's war raged on:

"Parlay!" Captain Whitey yelled. "I've got the goods!"

"Abort!" Moiler yelled, bouncing up and down.

"Take to the streets! Take to the streets!" Doctor Sunshine was so excited he flew away.

Captain Whitey ran with the bag of bread to the corner. He was flushed and sweaty. Doctor Sunshine flew back and landed on his shoulder. He spoke into Captain Whitey's ear. He said:

"Ah, man! Tough haul, tough haul."

"How many did we lose?" Captain Whitey was digging through the bread bag. He tore some bread up for the birds, he dropped it on the ground. He ate one loaf himself.

"Nobody lost, sir, Moiler's got a split lip, and Bunker's leg might be game, but all in all…"

"Not bad, is Bunker being taken care of?"

"Yes, sir."

"Drop the masts and anchor, I need some sleep. Give the men double rations."

"Yes, sir."

The parlay made Captain Whitey sad. He didn't like being so violent. He curled up inside the doorway to a building that had hundreds of tenants. He knew he would be woken up soon, if not sooner than he wanted to, but he was tired and sad. But what can you do? The sea is a violent mistress.

———

Even being sad, Captain Whitey slept well. He made a little hoop with his arms when he lay down on the doorstep. A little nest for the birds to sleep in. They all hopped upon him in excitement before going to bed. They pecked at his ears and cooed. His eyes were closed. He had a smile on his lips. The birds couldn't believe how successful they were. The injuries to Moiler and Bunker were minimal. Before long they were all sleeping silently in the hoop that Captain Whitey had made for them.

13

Morning came with a kick to Captain Whitey's back. A man in a suit was yelling:

"Get lost, you fucking bum!"

The birds had flown away the second the door opened. Captain Whitey rolled to the side and stood up. The man in the suit waited with his arms crossed until Captain Whitey took his cart and the bag of parlayed bread away. The man in the suit slapped his issue of the Times on his leg. "Fucking bums, make me so mad, draining our economy," the man mumbled. He was walking towards the train. Captain Whitey didn't care about the man and his politics, but he was a little confused about how the newspaper delivery was made without his notice. He must have been sleeping pretty hard, he decided. Or maybe pneumatic tubes, that would be cool!

Captain Whitey walked to the corner and sat down on the curb. The sun was coming up. Brooklyn was beginning to roil. He was thinking of pneumatic tubes delivering newspapers as he stacked the bread loafs on the sidewalk. He was fastidious with them in a way that you would probably treat bricks of gold. He counted them. Smelled them. Weighed them. He tore a chunk off one and tasted it, to make sure it was pure. The bread was pure. He smiled and stood up. He dug around in the trash can he was sitting next to and found a blood-encrusted feminine pad and a used condom. He sat down. Using the feminine pad as paper and the condom as a pen, the come inside the condom dripping out the tip, he wrote:

Day two. Just parlayed a feast of victual bounty! Moiler and Bunker, injured. The natives seemed terrified. Don't know if I have the heart to be a pirate. Feeling sad. Wonder what my mom would do.

Captain Whitey held the condom up to his lips like a pencil. Whoever's come that was in it dripped down his chin. His thoughts codified. He wrote:

The struggle is as hard as the goal.

Captain Whitey put the condom and the blood-soaked feminine

pad on the sidewalk. He felt profound. He wasn't profound though. He had read this stupid quote when he was at school. On a poster hanging in the hallway. He suddenly felt angry. Thankfully Bunker and Moiler flew down next to him before he brooded. Moiler said:

"Cappy!"

"Moiler, Bunker! Where are the rest of the goons?"

"Doctor Sunshine is taking a nap in the Associated parking lot, think Finch went over to the projects hoping to score, the stupid idiot. Detective Rabbi said he was gonna scout the canal for a new launch, and Beeper should be back soon. What happened with the suit man?"

"You're looking at it."

Bunker was pacing back and forth. He really wanted to say something. Captain Whitey waited a second, then said:

"What's on your mind, Bunker?"

"Fucking hell, why do you ask? I mean, hell. Why didn't you ask me before? You ever think of that? I mean, come on."

"Spit it out, or else!" Captain Whitey held up his fist. Bunker backed up.

"Sorry for living! You ever think of that? I mean, come on, give me a break. I am only trying to help, ever think of that?"

"Ok, Bunker, sorry, what's up?"

"Ok, good, glad you could see my point of view. But the answer is, nothing! Ha!" Bunker flew away. He pooped a turd onto the ground in defiance. Captain Whitey couldn't help but laugh. Moiler too. Captain Whitey said:

"That dude is a card! Talk to me, Moiler."

"What's the stacks?"

"Twelve French, twelve brown-grain seeders."

"They fit in the hold?"

"About to find out. We can cram them too. The weather is dry enough that we don't need to worry about spoilage. We should see what Doctor Sunshine has to say, but I think we are good for a fortnight."

"Meat and water?"

"Doctor Sunshine is waiting for us. We should move."

"Think you are right, there's Beeper. Let's haul ass."

14

Beeper flew down and landed on Captain Whitey's shoulder. Moiler hopped onto the top of the mail cart. Captain Whitey pushed the mail cart towards the parking lot of the the Associated market, where Doctor Sunshine was taking a nap. There must be water and meat there, Captain Whitey thought. The bread had been shoved into the mail cart. Captain Whitey and none of the birds knew how exactly. It had happened without thought. Nobody cared, but Captain Whitey who was trying his hardest to maintain control was baffled. It took him about two minutes to stop thinking about it, but when he stopped thinking about it he never thought about it again.

15

When they reached Doctor Sunshine he was carefully rested next to a car bumper on the edge of the parking lot. He was hungover and glassy-eyed. His eyes were deep in their sockets, and he looked soulful. He stretched his wings and yawned. A bird's yawn. Captain Whitey laughed. He said:

"Rough night?"

"Do they make other kinds?"

"Ha, not that I know of, not in America at least, Moiler says you got a stint on some beef?"

"I do. Over there." Doctor Sunshine pointed his beak at the dumpster by the recycling kiosks. Captain Whitey looked over. Moiler and Beeper had flown off. Captain Whitey sat down and leaned against the car bumper. He said:

"Good beef?"

"Great beef!"

"When?"

"Sundown, I suppose. Been watching for some time. Or, I guess, after dark."

Captain Whitey took a cardboard tube that once held paper towels from the side pocket of the mail cart. He held it up to his eye. He spied the dumpster. He brought it down. He said:

"There is a good perimeter if we hug the fence and attack from the west side. That concrete block might impede us a little, but we can navigate that, no problem. What do you think? Pitch here and wait? I could use some rest and we are well out of sight."

"Yes, rest. There is a patch of grass over there that only has two dog shits, and one is old and dry. Does the crew know where to meet us?"

"If they know what's good for them, they do. When Finch shows up I'll send the word."

Captain Whitey and Doctor Sunshine moved camp to the patch of grass on the edge of the parking lot that had only two pieces of dog shit. One wet and one dry. Captain Whitey flung both away with a stick he found. The dry one disintegrated. The wet one hit the chain-link fence and stuck. Captain Whitey threw the stick over the top of the fence and took some newspapers out and made himself a bed. It was going to be a long night. He needed some rest. He would nap for now. He would wait for word from Finch. Night was a long way off. The grass was soft. Captain Whitey put his back down on top of the papers. He put his hands underneath his head. He looked up at the clouds slinking by. They seemed embarrassed, like they were hiding something. Doctor Sunshine hopped on his chest. He was asleep in moments. Moments later, Captain Whitey was asleep too.

16

A chest full of birds. Captain Whitey woke to a chest full of birds. All asleep, the birds. Beeper, Bunker, Moiler, Detective Rabbi, Doctor Sunshine, Finch. And blackness. Night. Night was there. Captain Whitey startled himself. Shit. He sat up. The birds scattered. Shit. Did we miss it?

They didn't miss it. Captain Whitey took a moment to get his bearings. His eyes adjusted to the light in the parking lot. The birds flew back and landed at his feet. He was sitting with crossed legs. He scrambled over to the mail cart and took out his paper towel tube and spied the dumpster. He put it back. He said:

"All clear. Should we roll?"

"I think so, sir." Doctor Sunshine was ready.

"Ok, let's roll then, are we ready to roll?"

All the birds bobbed. Finch didn't because he wasn't a pigeon, but in his mind he did. Captain Whitey led the birds around the perimeter, along the fence, past the concrete obstruction and onto the dumpster full of beef.

The smell was awful. It smelled like death. The meat was bad. All of it. It was slimy and dripping. The birds flew away. Captain Whitey threw up. He heard a noise. Somebody was coming out the door by the dumpster. It was a man. He had a cigarette in his hand and a bag of rotten steaks in a bag. He yelled at Captain Whitey:

"Go'ne, get!"

Whitey ran away. Thank god, that was gross! he thought as he dove behind cars in the parking lot. He went back towards the camp. He had a smile on his face. That was pretty stupid he decided. He couldn't wait to talk about it with the rest of the birds. He had a nice thing happening. He felt included. He kind of suddenly felt like a bird.

17

When Captain Whitey got back to camp the birds were waiting for him. They were pensive. Brooding even. Almost dejected. He sat down amongst them and decided to tell them a story. The smell of the canal wafted through the air like a wary and slightly turned infection. Captain Whitey took the bag of bread and opened it. He took out a loaf. He waited for the birds to stop bobbing around. He slowly and methodically started to break chunks of bread from the loaf. He stacked them in piles. One pile for each bird. He was sitting cross legged. The birds were interested. They calmed down and stopped pacing and bobbing. Eventually they were all sitting in front of him casually pecking at the stacks of torn bread in front of themselves. Captain Whitey ripped a hank for himself and tore a bite off. He chewed slowly, thinking of how to start his story. Inspiration came when a car horn honk made the birds jump, followed by another sudden calm. Captain Whitey spoke:

"It was a night, just like tonight. The sound of a dump truck being thrown off the Empire State Building. Pee-wee had lost his bike. A man, known as Francis, had seen the value in its currency. But, Pee-wee, he was no man to be left alone, the way most men would suffer. He took the matter into his own hands, he knew the bike was lost, but not gone. But Pee-wee woke up one day to find that his bike was gone. On this day he had himself a breakfast. He knew it was Francis's birthday, but he didn't care for Francis. Then Pee-wee went to go to the bike store, where Dottie worked. He locked his bike up. But when he came out, his bike was gone. Then he went to fight Francis in a swimming pool. Then he went on a trip, because Francis had stolen his bike and had sold it. But then … he had to deal with some bikers, and he knocked the bikers' motorcycles over, but he did a dance first! And then he hitched a ride with a criminal and ended up washing some dishes. This is where he met Simone, who was French, and then Simone had a mean boyfriend who chased Pee-wee into a dinosaur, but then Pee-wee escaped and went to the Alamo, where there was no basement, so he went to Los Angeles and dressed as a nun and got his bike back and then interrupted a film shoot for a music video. But then he was in a movie and he gave the criminal a foot-long hot-dog with a metal file in it. And in the end he got on his bike and rode away into the sunset with Dottie!"

This was Captain Whitey's favorite story. The birds loved the story. Most of them were asleep by the end of the story. Captain Whitey finished his hank of bread and went to bed himself. The meat attack was a bust, tomorrow though, that is the best part of life, waiting for tomorrow, to see what comes. These were his thoughts as he drifted to sleep on top of his newspapers bed. Watching the planes fly over. Hearing the birds snore, and smelling the dirty disgusting oil-soaked water waft its noisy aroma into his nostrils. He could not have possibly been any happier.

18

Captain Whitey woke in the morning with Bunker bouncing on his chest. The sun was out and Captain Whitey had a hard-on that hurt himself, that reminded him he was a teenager. He needed release. He pushed Bunker off his chest and told him to get lost, he had some work to do. Work, meaning he needed to pearl the grass, as the saying goes. But Bunker didn't relent. He hopped back on Captain Whitey's chest and started talking:

"You know what I mean? Wake up Cappy, we're burning daylight, wakey wakey. Wake up! Why don't you wake up? Huh? Wakey wakey, you know what I mean? Know what I meant by that?"

"Jesus Christ, Bunker, what is it?!"

"What's that? Is that a diving board? Boing, boing." During the night Captain Whitey had got up to piss. He didn't zip his zipper back up when he was finished. His dick was out and about and full of glory. Bunker had hopped on top of it. He was bouncing up and down.

"Stop, Bunker, stop!"

"Stop what, sir? You know what I mean? Splash! Kapow! Boing!" The movement on Captain Whitey's erection made something happen. He didn't want it to happen, but it did. It knocked Bunker off his perch and left him saturated in something white and animal.

"What the hell? What the hell! That's a terrible diving board!" Bunker was confused. Captain Whitey wasn't any more cognizant than Bunker, but he did feel a little better.

He said:

"Sorry, Bunker, I told you to stop."

"Yeah, well, I mean, you know what I mean?" Bunker slunk off and pecked on his feathers. Captain Whitey laughed a little. Bunker couldn't possibly clean himself without, you know, eating the, he just couldn't. Captain Whitey zipped his pants up.

It was now morning. And there was work to do.

19

The juicy sun sprayed its warm and moist tendrils upon the earth as Captain Whitey prepared for the day. He folded newspapers and organized hanks of bread. The birds bobbed around a fire cooking worms on sticks and drinking muddy water from the nearby gutter, calling it coffee. Captain Whitey was walking down to the canal to wash his crotch and face when he saw something he didn't expect. A woman. A woman of pure beauty with curly locks of rusty hair. His heart stopped. He stopped because his heart had stopped. It took a minute to catch his breath.

Enter the dame, he thought as he watched her squatting next to the canal, rinsing her illustrious woman-ness in the turbid greasy fountain lapping at the shore of her contingence. The burlap sack she wore as a dress made tertiary rainbows in Captain Whitey's eyes. There was a pigeon on each of her shoulders. A cake of bird shit covered her back. He wanted to approach her. He felt naked though. He ran back to the mail cart and grabbed some victuals.

He practiced some lines in his head as he approached her. Holding the bread out in his imaginary mind. He said suave things, like, "Well, hello, me lady, when did you get here?" Shit, no! "Well, hi, nice sack." Oh, hell no! "Hey baby, come here often? Want a hank of victuals?"

His one-liners didn't get to get used though. She approached him first. She said:

"Gimme that!" She took the hank of bread and used it to wipe her crotch. She tore the bread into pieces and threw them on the ground. Her birds flew from her shoulders and started to peck about. Captain Whitey was staring at her crotch. Her rusty pubes glistened in greasy grandeur. She blushed. She seemed like she was wearing too much blush. Captain Whitey didn't know about makeup, so this confused him. He said:

"Why are you wearing so much blush?"

She blushed even more. This confused Captain Whitey. How did she get even more blush, he thought. She pulled her burlap dress down, covering her woman things. Captain Whitey didn't realize it, but he was pushing his erect manhood from the backside of his trousers. She looked at it. He became hot in the face. He put his hands over his crotch and smiled. He said:

"Sorry, ma'am, sometimes I get these boners."

"Don't be sorry, that's a nice boner, one time I saw a boner so big it could almost whack the moon! That was a bad boner."

"The moon?! I would like to see that!"

"Yeah, it was pretty cool."

"You come here often?" Captain Whitey got so embarrassed by saying this he ran away. He went and hid behind a tree. He watched the woman gather her things and walk off. The birds finished the bread and flew towards where she went. Captain Whitey's heart was racing. He had fallen in love.

20

When the woman was out of sight Captain Whitey made his way back to camp. His face had an imprint of the tree trunk he had been standing behind. He didn't realize he had been pushing his cheek against the bark. He was so engrossed his neck hurt. He had a dazed look in his eyes as he came upon the pigeons cleaning up their breakfast. Doctor Sunshine was the first to notice, he said:

"Jesus, Cappy, what the fuck?"

"I'm in love, Doctor Sunshine, in love!"

"But how? You were just washing your balls, how do you fall in love washing your balls?"

"I don't know, but I did."

"Does she have nice wings?"

"Beautiful, wonderful wings!"

"And beak? Does she have a nice beak?"

"The most amazing beak! And feathers like cool cut glass! I couldn't be more happier!"

"Oh Jesus, man!"

Doctor Sunshine slapped Captain Whitey in the face with his wing tip. He yelled:

"Pull your shit together, man! We got work to do! We should be shipping off by the fortnight!"

"I know, I know, but the heart needs to wander, like stars in a Mercury night!"

"Your thoughts are diarrhea! Stop it, man!"

"Like the other moon, the one from the mountain!"

"Fuck your poetry, you need counsel. Take a nap. I'm gonna rally the troops, you better not be like this when I get back."

"There is no harp that goes as deep as the lanyard of love!"

"Pffft."

Doctor Sunshine stormed off leaving Captain Whitey to his musings of love things. This was not part of the plan, Doctor Sunshine thought as he packed his pipe. When he got to the other birds, he said in an annoyed voice:

"Give me a match!"

21

Captain Whitey mused for quite some time. He had never been in love before. He felt great. The dirty ditch that was the canal suddenly smelled like a rose under a heat lamp. His toes were tingling. His appetite resumed. He ate a loaf of victuals with his eyes closed, musing:

"My earth, my grateful, bendy earth. To roll you one more time, just tonight. To sleep, to dream no more!"

Captain Whitey took a twig from the ground and an empty juice container he found lying in the grass beside him and wrote in his log:

"Day Four. Found love. Victuals are abounding. Weather seems steady. Men are asking where the beef is. Failed endeavor. I want beef too. Where exactly is the beef? I am hoping the morning will have the answer. Feeling like a landlubber. The men are getting restless."

Captain Whitey put his log down. He sighed as he got into bed. Bed, meaning lying down on his newspapers. He crossed his arms and stared into the starry sky. He thought about the woman with the burlap sack and her birds on her shoulders and the white bird shit caked on her back. He fell asleep with a smile on his face.

22

The morning was a mist of sorts. It was almost raining. Captain Whitey woke up shivering. Doctor Sunshine was standing next to him, waiting. He said:

"You awake?"

"I am now, thanks." Captain Whitey sat up.

"Fuck it, let's roll."

"Fine, ok, fine. Let me pack my shit." Captain Whitey rolled his newspapers bed up. He crammed it into the side of the mail cart.

"You guys get breakfast?"

"Bunker found some worms."

"He clean himself up? Poor dog." Captain Whitey crammed the bread, the victuals, into the other side of the mail cart.

"He's fine. Still doesn't understand why you did that, think you owe him an apology."

"Yeah, well, I told him that shit ain't a goddamned springboard. Think instead he owes me an apology, lucky I don't make him walk the plank."

"He already did, sir."

"Fuck off. Leave me. I got business."

Doctor Sunshine hopped off towards the other birds. They were packing their things, meaning they were hopping around and cooing. Captain Whitey went over to the canal and made a certain business. He used the oily water to wash the valve of his errant restriction. He laughed as he watched it float away. "Torpedo!" he yelled.

The birds flew up in the air because of his exclamation. He laughed at this too. Those fickle jerks, he thought, what a life to live! I could never be so skittish. A dog barked nearby. He pulled his pants up quickly. He suddenly felt embarrassed. He was just as bad as them.

Captain Whitey went back to the mail cart and whistled. The birds flew over. They landed on his shoulders and also on top of the mail cart. They were ready to go, to parlay, to find the beef. The air felt wet and heavy. Captain Whitey pushed into it, to what felt like fog, but was only mist. Today we are wet, he thought, but by tonight, tonight, we sleep in a dry castle with marble walls and beef galore! He said:

"Parlay!" The birds did their best to scream. But it was only cooing. Captain Whitey pushed them through the fog/mist.

23

The bare branches of a pear tree, the Christmas that never existed, the mind of a bouillant euchre, lay my hand down, I swear, I will know the answer. Captain Whitey pushed through the fog. The mist. Doctor Sunshine was on his shoulder. Doctor Sunshine. He kept biting on his beard. Captain Whitey's. Picking hairs loose and letting them drop. The hairs collected on Whitey's arm, on the crook of his elbow. Captain Whitey yanked his head away every time this happened. It felt like a pinch. He said:

"Knock it off! That hurts."

"Grow a blower, butter breath, need an orange?"

"What? I'm scurvy? Like hell! Eat one yourself!"

"I'll eat one when you make one!"

The smell of hot-dogs stopped them in their tracks. The man with the hot-dog cart, next to the park. Captain Whitey wondered if he had hot-dog money. The phrase, "One footlong…," came to mind. He dug around in his pockets. Nothing was doing. He made a face like Napoleon and shook his head:

"We are broke, Doctor Sunshine, we must prevail instead."

"Parlay, you mean."

"Yes, parlay!"

The man with the hot-dogs watched as Captain Whitey talked to the birds. This made Captain Whitey nervous. He ran off, pushing the mail cart. Doctor Sunshine flew away. The man with the hot-dogs just shook his head. Parlaying was hard. Captain Whitey hid behind a dumpster. He waited for Doctor Sunshine to come back. And also Detective Rabbi, he needed a voice of reason, maybe two voices of reason. They never showed up. He pushed his mail cart onto the sidewalk and walked away.

An hour went by. Captain Whitey found himself bored and alone. He was hungry now and gnawing on a hank of bread. He had wandered into a deeper part of Brooklyn, alone and loose. He wondered:

"Where are those fuckers at?"

Captain Whitey took out his paper towel tube and scanned the skyline. There was no birds to be seen. He rubbed his back against the brick wall he was leaning against. His back was itchy. He felt like a bear. He was sitting down. He thought:

"Get real for once."

This made him feel like a boner. He laughed to himself. He laid his head back. He didn't mean to, but he took a nap.

24

The nap took an hour. He woke up because he was being bitten by a mosquito. He scratched his arm. He rubbed his eyes. He stood up. Captain Whitey took his paper towel tube and scoured the sky. No birds. Where are those fuckers? he thought. A ship needs a crew to parlay, he thought. Suck it, he thought. He stood up and pushed his mail cart down the sidewalk.

On the corner of the street he looked into the trash can. There wasn't a single victual. He did find some napkins and a used tea bag. The tag read: English Breakfast Tea. Fancy, he thought. He tore the string off so he could practice his knots. He put the bag in his pocket thinking the birds might fancy a cup of tea on the long nights out on the drink. The string he wrapped around his finger. The tag he tore off with his teeth and chewed on the paper. When it became a ball he spit it at a squirrel that was climbing a tree nearby. He missed, but this reminded him about having weapons. He dug around in the trash can until he found a piece of paper that read: New Saigon Delivery Menu. Saigon, shit, he thought. Captain Whitey tore the menu into strips. He tore the strips into pieces. He put the pieces into his pocket. He decided he should go back to camp. He took one last look through his paper towel tube. No birds. He put it away, along with the napkins. He disembarked.

The walk back to camp was slow and tedious, lacking in parlay. No victuals, no birds. He felt dejected by the time he reached camp. His spirits were lifted though when he saw all the birds were waiting for him. They were playing rummy. Yelling at each other. They were drunk. He parked the mail cart and sat down in their circle. He said:

"Deal me in."

"Sure thing Cappy, you old coot! Where ya been? We been waiting." Doctor Sunshine was dealing.

"Waiting for me, ha! I been waiting for you fuckers for like hours, where the hell you been?"

"We been here. Holding down the fort, well not Bunker, he has news, Bunker, you wanna tell him or should I?"

"What do you mean? I mean, I will tell him, you know what I mean? I mean…"

The birds and Captain Whitey sat in a circle. There were chunks of paper in the middle. The card game. Captain Whitey sat cross-legged with a huge smile on his face. He loved these guys. He wasn't mad that they ditched him. Bunker lit his pipe and started his story:

"So, I mean, just like that, I mean, I was flying around, minding my own business, like ya know, I mean, and then there was this guy, let me tell you, this guy, fucking hell, just like that, throwing seed on the ground! You know what I mean, grade A feed, just like that, on the ground! And so, what do I do? What would you do? I mean, you know what I mean, I dove down, and sure as shit the shit was grade A shit! And there I am, munching on this sweet-ass grub and I see this dame, gams to the ceiling, summer dress and all, flowing like a cotton blowhole, you see? See what I mean? Thar she blows, I mean, and there I am just cramming grade A morsels in my mouth, and sure as shit, she walks over me. And shiver me timbers! The dame was naked as a purloined cat underneath that dress! I saw it all! Just like that! My beak dropped to the ground! You could park a ship inside, you could, I was so flabbergasted. I mean, I stood there in shock. I had to go run into the bushes, you know what I mean, I couldn't take it. Gams like mountains."

"Fucking perv." Moiler laughed.

"That's pretty dirty, Bunker." Captain Whitey was laughing too.

The game started again and everybody started yelling at each other. The idea of parlaying drifted into the distance. The birds and Captain Whitey played cards until sundown. Then they built a fire. Everybody was drunk in the end, including Captain Whitey. They sang songs about the sea and told stories about the things they had seen. Every single one of them went to bed happy, especially Captain Whitey. He felt a searing earnestness when he thought about it. These are his people, he decided, these birds, they get it.

After declaring his love for each and every one of them, Captain Whitey passed out with his head on a rock. A pillow. The fire died down eventually. The pigeons all slept on top of him. He was at peace in such a deep way that the only indication he wasn't dead was the smile on his face as he slept.

25

The morning light fell brutal on Captain Whitey's face. His head hurt. He opened his eyes and moaned. There was drool on his pillow. The rock. The sun felt like a blanket of heat. The pigeons were up and moving about. Hungover as well. Smoke leaked from the ashes of the bonfire from t he n ight b efore. T he b irds s tumbled a round, making coffee and dozing. Smoking pipes and merrymaking. There was a lot of coughing. Farting. Vomiting. The dirt that Captain Whitey was lying on felt like impacted clay. He tried to keep sleeping, but there was nothing doing, the day was too hot, and the birds were too noisy. He was also thirsty. And needed to piss. He stood up. Detective Rabbi said, "Morning, Cap. Chipper are we?" and giggled.

"Blow it, Detective Rabbi."

"It ain't my fault." Detective Rabbi put his head under his wing.

"Sorry, yes, just gotta pee. Fucking hell, what did we do to ourselves?"

"A man, as always, Cappy, who can know what darkness, right?" Detective Rabbi had taken his head from under his wing and smiled at Captain Whitey.

"Always a poet, you lift my spirit, but now, to the latrine!"

"Always the answer, sir. You inspire."

"And always the question, can you, in fact, suck it, mate?"

"Here, here!" They both laughed.

"Ok, I'm off. Don't take any wooden nickels."

"I won't, sir. Don't forget to wipe."

"Duly noted."

Captain Whitey went down to the canal to piss. The sun made his dick hot. There were some tourists on the other side of the canal that became scandalized. They were women. Three of them. They put their hands to their mouths, but watched him pee. Oh, grow up, Captain Whitey thought as he shook his dick at them. He wasn't in the mood for polite society. He had victuals needing and hardtack and the crew was wonderfully hungover. It's that kind of day, he thought as he put his dick back into his pants. He zipped his zipper. He needed some water. He made his way to the water fountain by the entrance to the park. But then, just like that, he saw her again.

The woman in the burlap sack. Rusty hair and covered in bird shit. Love. She was washing her panties in the drinking fountain. Captain Whitey couldn't take it. He ran and hid behind a tree. He peeked around it. She was wringing out her panties on the ground. She draped them on the edge of a park bench. She pulled up her skirt and put her left foot on top of the concrete column. Her shoes were boots. Whitey watched her as she exposed her hairy womanness to the open air. She used one hand to push the button that made the water come out of the spigot. The other hand she used to splash water on her femininity. She rubbed herself clean. Then she adjusted herself and cleaned her hind areas. Captain Whitey couldn't take it. He was so manly that he could chop down the tree he was standing behind. It took all of one touching to set him off. He crumpled to the ground in ecstasy. The noise made the woman look up. She saw him laid out on the ground, agonizing. She smiled. Captain Whitey tried to hide, but there was no use. He stood up. Gathered himself. And like a true gentleman, he walked over to her.

She was done washing. She was putting her wet panties back on as Captain Whitey got within talking distance. He stumbled, holding out his hand, saying:

"I'm Whitey, lady." His voice squeaked. He was about to turn around and run away, but she spoke.

"I'm Runa, don't be shy. I've been thinking about that boner of yours. You look a little wet." Runa looked at his crotch. Captain Whitey looked down. His manliness had spoiled his trousers.

"Oh, that, ma'am, some kid threw a water balloon, sorry, ma'am."

"Oh kids, they can be awful. What happened to your boner? It seems to have gone away."

"I'm sure it will be back, knock on wood." Captain Whitey smiled. He thought he was being funny. His head started to spin and he wanted to run away again. Then his boner returned.

"Oh, there it is! Can I touch it?"

Captain Whitey took his penis out. His pants dropped to the

ground. Runa approached him. Her burlap sack scratched against his marbled ruins. She put her hands on the place of new dawns. Her hands were cold and she smelled like pigeon shit and lilac. Captain Whitey expressed himself in a fountain of deliverance. Runa laughed. "You're so sensitive," she said. Captain Whitey's eyes went white and he pulled up his pants. He ran away as fast as he could.

Captain Whitey ran and hid behind a car. He buckled his belt. He peaked over to watch her some more, but she was gone. He slid down. Looking at the sky he repeated her name, "Runa, Runa." He almost started crying he was so much in love. Arrgh, what have I gotten myself into, he thought. He sat there trying to think thoughts for some time. But the thoughts never came. He had to punch himself in the face to stop thinking of her. It didn't work, but he was able to put her to the side enough to stand up and head back to camp.

<h1 style="text-align:center">26</h1>

When Captain Whitey got back to camp he found it in disarray. There was a scuffle in progress. Detective Rabbi and Bunker were rolling around on the ground. There was a cloud of dust. The rest of the birds were egging them on. Moiler was screaming:

"Get his leg! Get his fucking leg!" Detective Rabbi reached for Bunker's leg. They both stumbled, Bunker threw himself back and pulled out a knife. Detective Rabbi rolled to his side and stood up, his wings extended like a wrestler ready to pounce. They bounced around each other in a circle. Bunker stabbing at the air between them. Detective Rabbi jumping back each time. Captain Whitey jumped into the mix and wrestled the knife from Bunker. He screamed:

"Give it up, Bunker, Rabbi is a damned dirty cat! He'll ream you as sure as he knows your junker!"

"Fuck that rat! Fuck that dying rat!" Bunker let the knife go, not without resistance, but he knew he was beat. Captain Whitey stood between the two, making sure they didn't attack each other anymore. Detective Rabbi backed off. Bunker was taken away by Finch and Moiler. Doctor Sunshine put the tips of his wings on Detective Rabbi's shoulders. The scene calmed down. Captain Whitey was panting. He handed the knife to Doctor Sunshine. He slid it into his belt. Detective Rabbi looked insane. After a moment he calmed down. He didn't look so insane anymore. Captain Whitey said:

"Sunshine, give Bunker his knife back, tell him I'll talk to him later."

"Yes, sir. But I gotta tell you." Doctor Sunshine had a look on his face.

"Later, Sunshine. Do as you're told, I need a minute with Rabbi, point."

"Yes, sir." Doctor Sunshine took the knife and walked away. He stopped. Turning around, he almost said, "But I" but he didn't. He kept walking. Captain Whitey watched him go. He then turned to Detective Rabbi. He said:

"What the hell, mate? He was gonna gut ye?"

"Ah, Cappy, I sure am sorry, but you gotta understand." Detective Rabbi became very sensitive. He almost started weeping. He sucked it up. Captain Whitey waited. Detective Rabbi chewed on his beak. He said:

"He called me a lubber. That motherfucker called me a lubber. Me! A lubber!"

"I am sure…"

"I have never lubbed in my life! Three generations my family oils, my Grandpapa was born with a bowlined umbilical chord! The doctor cut him loose with a liver wrench! My Great-Grandpapa smacked him in the face and said: You idiot! Don't you know that knot? You don't need a knife! Lubber! That doctor was a lubber! Not me, never a lubber. You call me a lubber, you will get a liver wrench of your own!"

"Yeah, but it's Bunker, you know Bunker, he says things."

"My ass says things, but it don't mean I need to take it."

"Yeah, you gonna fight your own ass?"

"Fucking hell, good point, fuck off Cappy," Detective Rabbi smiled. "You got a point."

"We got a good ship, mate. I'll teach Bunker a bowline, you get some rest, take this." Captain Whitey unraveled the tea string from around his finger. "I'll make Bunker practice on reeds."

"You're a good man, Captain Whitey." He tucked the string under his wing.

"We'll see about that." Captain Whitey smiled and walked away.

27

Bunker was next to a rock crying. Finch and Moiler had flown off. Bunker was blubbering to himself:

"I mean, what did I ever do to hurt somebody's feelings. Nothing I tell you, I mean, nothing." Captain Whitey sat down next to Bunker. He put his arm around him. He felt sad for poor Bunker. He talked so much because he wanted to be understood, but nobody understood him. They called him a motormouth, the dribbler dictator, pants on a fence, which confused Captain Whitey until he realized that hanging pants on a fence meant doing the job twice. A fence on a fence. Captain Whitey thought for a second that he should rename Bunker, Fencer, but then this confusion would just make things more complicated. Talker, Bunker, Fencer, too much. Bunker fit, so he let it fit. Captain Whitey said:

"Oh Bunker, it's ok. Detective Rabbi isn't mad at you."

"But he is, sir, you know what I mean? I mean, he tried to punch my lights out. You know what I mean? I did call him a lubber."

"But it doesn't matter Bunker, he loves you and didn't mean it. I think you guys can talk and figure it out."

"But I mean, I don't take it back though. I saw him lub, I did, I did, I can prove it!"

"Detective Rabbi ain't a lubber, leave it alone, man, he knows more seas than Poseidon, I've seen that rank buckler tie a knot so hard even God couldn't untie it!"

"You sure?"

"I am certain, Bunker. Rest assured."

"I trust you Cappy, I hope you mean it."

"I mean it, Bunker."

Bunker stopped crying. He hugged Captain Whitey on the leg. He flew away. Captain Whitey sat there wondering what the hell his crew was up to. He smiled and felt happy. The smell of the canal wafted to his nose. The day was calling. He stood up and made his way back to camp. All the fires were out and the pigeons were gone. Finch was gone too. He peeked around to make sure Runa was gone as well. She made him so nervous. She was gone. He sighed. He kind of wished she wasn't gone all of a sudden. He ran over and punched a tree to make his thoughts go away. This only gave him a boner because he was thinking of her. He did a weird dance around the camp hoping to alleviate the pressure. It was an actual dance. He unzipped his pants and let his boner breathe air. He flapped his arms. He ran down to the canal and splashed water on his face. He ran back to the camp and punched his dick side to side. He screamed out, "La loo loo, la loo loo!" The boner stayed. And now it hurt.

He was about to go into the bushes and whack his penchant shorewise when a bird with incredibly long legs flew down and met him in his fevered compunction. The bird said:

"I like your moves. Don't mean to interrupt, but I think you might be dancing alone." Captain Whitey's boner deflated. He tucked it back into his pants and zipped his zipper.

"Yeah, no, just having some problems, since when are you an expert?"

"Expert, no!"

"Then what the fuck, you don't know how to mind your own business?"

"What business, I am just trying to say hi." The stork turned to the side a little, he thought he was being clever, but suddenly realized he was being crass.

"Hi, bye." Captain Whitey started to pick up all of his things and parlay.

"No, no, no, no! Don't leave, I've been watching you guys, I want to join. I know a place. Not far from here, gutters of hot-dogs and bins of bread, you gotta trust me!" Captain Whitey stopped packing. He erected himself and turned around.

"Talk to me."

"Soccer park, over by the promenade."

"Keep talking."

"Every night at the kiosk they throw a bag or two at least of victuals and vestments! I swear by my life! Don't believe me, come tonight."

"When?"

"Ten."

"We'll see, who do we ask for?"

"Maurice, or Daddy Long Legs, I will tell them you are coming."

"You're Daddy Long Legs, I suppose?"

"Gams like mountains!"

"Son of a bitch, you have been watching!" Daddy Long Legs flew away laughing. Captain Whitey laughed too. Vestments and victuals sounded great. He would rest and wait for the crew to get back from their doings. He smelled a banana peel. His boner returned. He had no choice but to run to the bushes and whack off. He was already sick of being in love, but he reasoned that if it felt like this all the time he could compensate. He fell asleep thinking of new philosophies.

28

The new philosophy was simple: Love. And all it stands for.

When Captain Whitey woke up he reached for a leaf and a twig. He started writing furiously:

Day what, I don't know, seven? I thought I had a grip on things, but now I am not so sure. A tempest has taken over camp. Detective Rabbi and Bunker are fighting. Finch is showing signs of the drippings. I think Doctor Sunshine is mad at me. Moiler seems fine, but you can never tell with him, he sometimes brings me soup, but forgets the spoon. I think it might be on purpose. He doesn't talk. I have watched him sharpen his knife. The look in his eye seems important. Beeper seems fine too, but I think he is having nightmares, in the morning he has dark circles under his eyes and he seems to have trouble with breakfast. Weather is holding. I am praying for more sun. If we can leave before the season begins I will give the men a extra doubloon. This man, Daddy Long Legs, seems to know a thing or two about victuals and something he calls vestments, I don't know what that means, but he seems to be trustworthy. This woman Runa seems to have put a dent in the hull. I want to drop my anchor inside of her. I have yet to meet her crew, or even heard about her voyage. This makes me nervous. She hasn't asked me either about my finger or my designs. She touched my boner though. I think this makes me happy. Only time will tell. I hear of oil on the south shore now. There is talk in the taverns of shifting airs. I refuse to listen to such gossip, but I constantly worry. Are we already too late? If we don't breach quick, I feel I may explode. My patience is dwindling.

Captain Whitey threw the twig and leaf on the ground. He stood up and gathered his things. He smiled like a gassy pig and pushed the mail cart towards the docks. He whistled as loud as he could. Nobody came. His crew was officially bunked. They needed a talking to. He crossed the canal. Near the grocery store. A block later he was covered in birds. Moiler and Bunker and Beeper rode on the mail cart. Detective Rabbi and Doctor Sunshine rode on his shoulders. Finch dug himself into one of his pockets and squirmed. They had heard his call. They were ready for action. They all looked forward. Scanning the distance. Hooked hands, pegged legged, pipes and eye patches. Captain Whitey pushed on. Business.

About two blocks later, as they were approaching Atlantic Avenue, Finch started wriggling uncontrollably. Captain Whitey became distracted. He stopped the procession. He reached into his pocket and pulled Finch out. Finch's eyes were wild and itchy. He writhed in Captain Whitey's hand. Captain Whitey said:

"What's up Finch, you seem in pain."

"I am, Cappy, I think the night girls did me wrong! I can't! I can't… get the relief."

"Let me see." Captain Whitey spread Finch's tiny legs and looked at his tiny genitals. They were bright red and choked with puss. "Oh Jesus, hold on, Moiler, Detective Rabbi, come hold his wings." Moiler and Detective Rabbi flew up onto Captain Whitey's hand. They grabbed his wings and held him down. Finch screamed.

"What the hell are you doing!"

"Relax, this will only take a second." Captain Whitey smiled at Detective Rabbi. He smiled back. "You're gonna feel a pinch." Captain Whitey used his thumb to pop the puss from Finch's genitals. Puss went everywhere. Both Moiler and Detective Rabbi tucked their heads to the side. Captain Whitey laughed and got some in his mouth. Finch flew away. Captain Whitey spit on the ground. It smelled like green oranges. He laughed again and said:

"Let this be a lesson to you."

Nobody learned a lesson. Moiler lit a pipe. Detective Rabbi adjusted his eye patch. Beeper grimaced. Doctor Sunshine frowned, and Bunker muttered into his armpit. This all brought brightness to Captain Whitey's eyes. He announced a break, and took victuals from the mail cart. He smiled and threw chunks of bread onto the ground. The birds jumped down and started eating. In his mind though, they were wearing tuxedos. Drinking champagne. He stood there proud, a member of the yacht club. He looked around for a while, then sat down on a bench. He would wait for Finch to come back. There was sun on his skin and a bench on his back. He closed his eyes and listened. This was good. In fact, better than good, this was great!

<h1 style="text-align:center">29</h1>

The day absorbed the sunlight. Careful soft babies of shade cooed as time roiled into the future. The pigeons napped. Captain Whitey napped. Finch came back and napped too. At dusk a new excitement arose. Nobody said anything. They all, the pigeons and Captain Whitey, rose and prepared themselves. They had no idea if they were meeting friends or harbingers. They were preparing for battle, just in case.

Captain Whitey tied a plastic bag across his forehead. He felt like a samurai. He folded it in a way that when he put it on, it read: Key Food. He was certain he looked badass. He did some karate moves to prove his point. The birds all talked in hushes. They were applying face paint. Finch got scared and got back into Captain Whitey's pocket. Captain Whitey patted the pocket and said, "There, there." This calmed Finch down. He fell asleep.

The pigeons had one more smoke. "One for the road," Moiler said as he lit his pipe, "could be the last." "Here, here," the other pigeons said. They all took a shot of rum and gathered around Captain Whitey. Captain Whitey did his best to look confident, but he was scared too. He stood as erect as he could. He said:

"I don't ask much from you men, but tonight I might ask for all. A man is not made by his thoughts, nor his actions, no, my charges, a man is made by his heart! If your heart is not in this we must not proceed, for an uncertain heart is worse than a dubious heart. If you feel dubious, I can let you go, but if you are uncertain, well, man, you become a liability. All men must know destiny the way all soldiers must know death, there is no easy day but yesterday. Let us pray our enemy die quickly and with little pain, and may their women and children bask in the glory that their death shall bring!"

"Here, here!"

The speech was so moving that the birds immediately flew away. Captain Whitey yelled:

"No, no, come back!" But it was too late. Only Finch remained.

Snoring in his pocket. Captain Whitey took the mail cart and pushed on towards the kiosk by the soccer courts.

80 Parlay

Snoring in his pocket. Captain Whitey took the mail cart and pushed on towards the kiosk by the soccer courts.

30

The light outside the kiosk was a street lamp. Nobody was there to greet him. The silence was unnerving. He approached the dumpster with caution. The lid was down. He crept to the dumpster and listened for a while. He heard nothing. He lifted the lid slightly. He could smell victuals. He looked around and then threw the lid open completely. Two ravens flew out and attacked him. He ran away and jumped behind a bench leaving his mail cart behind. The ravens flew back to the dumpster and went back inside. They somehow closed the lid. Captain Whitey's heart was beating fast. He was crouched. Finch woke up and fluttered to his shoulder and shook like a bird, he whispered in Captain Whitey's ear:

"Fuck, Cappy, what's up?"

"Shush."

"What happened?" Finch whispered softer.

"They're on to us, shush, stay here, I'm gonna poke around the corner and have a look-see." Finch hopped on the back of the bench and took look-out. Captain Whitey crouched down and snuck past the bench. He gave Finch the eye-to-eye. Finch nodded. Captain Whitey disappeared into the darkness. A moment went by. He came back. Finch was shivering in fear. Captain Whitey said in a hushed voice:

"Ok, we're cool. They don't got any men on the perimeter. Go get those dickweeds, but be quiet about it."

"Ok, but what's up?"

"It was a set-up! A trap. Do as you're told."

Finch flew off to find the crew. He was so upset that he shit ten times. He could barely gather the words to tell the pigeons when he found them bouncing around on the corner of Atlantic and Court that they needed to haul ass. Captain Whitey needed them. They flew off immediately. Finch flew away because he was still scared. He found a tree with a nice hole and took it over for the night.

When the birds landed next to Captain Whitey he still had his eye on the dumpster outside the kiosk by the soccer court. He was crouched. He didn't look at them he was so focused. But he whispered:

"Fuckers, where'd you go? Not important, see that?"

"The dumpster?" Detective Rabbi jumped on his shoulder.

"Yeah, yeah. Two ravens inside acting like barn swallows with babies. Think we can get them though, it's a trap though, keep waiting for Daddy Long Legs to show, he must be near, waiting to pounce."

"Fuck, is it worth it?"

"I think it might be, ideas?"

"The ship is there, waiting, I say we just parlay, fuck them bitches."

"Ok, I agree, I will lead the charge, when the ravens fly out you guys attack, when Daddy Long Legs shows up I'll punch him in the gizzard. Plan?"

"Plan."

Detective Rabbi hopped down and gave the orders. Captain Whitey gathered his nerve. A minute went by. He stood up and ran, yelling:

"Parlay!"

Captain Whitey threw the lid up. The ravens erupted. The crew descended upon them. There was an air battle. Squawks were everywhere. Screeches. Captain Whitey grabbed as many victuals as he could. Suddenly there was a shadow from the streetlight and Daddy Long Legs descended. He knocked all the pigeons out of the air. They fell to the ground. He started attacking Captain Whitey who was putting the victuals in the mail cart. The ravens were stunned and rolling around on the ground. Captain Whitey was punching the air behind him as he ran away. The pigeons were attacking Daddy Long Legs, who had his talons in Captain Whitey's back. Captain Whitey tried to punch his neck. Daddy Long Legs gave up and flew off. Captain Whitey pushed the mail cart as fast as he could down the street. The pigeons flew off in a fluster. The smell of war was acrid as Captain Whitey dove behind an orange construction barrel. He was out of breath and white in the eye. His fists were cocked and waiting for another attack. The attack never came. He caught his breath, waiting, watching. He could feel blood running down his back. The smell of new asphalt consumed him as he wondered about the fate of his men.

31

Captain Whitey limped his way back to camp. The blood coagulated on his back. It was itchy as it scabbed. He was livid. That stupid fucking bird, he thought as he walked, pushing the mail cart, fool me once, fuck you, he thought. Fool me twice, a pox on your house.

Camp was bustling when Captain Whitey got there. The birds were in high spirits and drinking. Moiler was playing a lute and singing a dirge. The lyrics were dirty. Whitey smiled. He was received with a hero's welcome. "Cappy!" they yelled. Moiler smiled at him, but didn't stop singing:

"A penny for your thoughts, a nickel for your kickers, roll me over lubber and remove your knickers. I came here once, I came here twice, I don't like gambling, but I roll the dice. Venereal, my sweet, sweet, venereal... disease."

Captain Whitey forgot about his troubles. He parked the mail cart and sat down with the birds. He joined in, into the chorus, "Venereal, my sweet, sweet, venereal... disease." There was a bonfire burning and the night had a myriad of stars. Ten thousand and one to be precise. Captain Whitey counted them. He was good at counting stars. His eyesight was excellent. He also was good at counting things. But there was no actual way he counted all those stars. He laid back and fell asleep, happy to be surrounded by the people he loved.

Halfway through the night he woke up. Runa was pushing on his chest. He almost punched her, thinking she was an enemy. But when he realized she wasn't, his dick became hard. The smell of her breath. He said:

"Shit, Runa. What the hell?"

"I want you inside me."

"Um, ok." She pulled his pants down, he smelled like a barbed wire fence. She pulled her pants off. She smelled like rusty tetanus as her nature slid down his ebullient roister. She kissed him in shatters. She came in seconds. She stood up and left, dragging her pants behind her as she made her way back to her own camp. Captain Whitey said:

"What the fuck?"

He paused for a second. His dick hurt. His balls were screaming. He masturbated to the universe. There was so much come that he didn't know how to deal with it. He rolled over and let the earth deal with it all. Clods of come gathered around his privates. He would deal with this in the morning.

32

In the morning Captain Whitey was stuck to the ground. He had to peel himself up. His dick got longer and longer before it snapped away from the ground and returned to his body. He rubbed his belly and pulled up his pants. He hated being in love with this girl, she was bad news, but he wanted to see her again, now, and as soon as possible.

All the birds were gone, including Finch. Captain Whitey was not surprised. They were a fickle crew. He got up and went to the canal to clean himself. He found Runa there with both of her birds. His heart shook a little, like a single raisin in a cardboard box. He approached her, slowly. He didn't want her to know that he loved her. But she sucked him in. She was a vacuum of beauty. He tried to play it cool. He said:

"Yo, Runa, like, what's the haps?" He almost ran away he was so embarrassed.

"Oh, hey, Whitey." She didn't care, she was slapping the water, trying to make a fish appear.

"That was cool last night, I liked it, I think, I mean..." He almost ran away again.

"Oh, yeah, right, I suppose, you ever meet these two? Princess Toots and Maybellene?"

"No, not yet. Hi, girls." The pigeons nodded, or bobbed their heads.

"Yeah, they're cool, what'cha doing?"

"I don't know, gonna wash this come off, you?"

"Oh, I don't know, fishing maybe, ok, smell you later." Runa wandered off. Princess Toots and Maybellene followed. Captain Whitey stood there confused. He went down to the canal and rinsed the come and dirt from his belly. The water was greasy and not kind. It burned slightly. He felt used and unhappy. He sat down on the edge of the canal to think. No real thoughts came. In his head the phrase, "Maybe she was born with it, maybe it's Maybellene," repeated over and over. Followed by, "Princess Toots? A farting royalty? A royal bird? As if! Where do they find these people? I never!"

The thoughts drifted away as easily as the water that made the canal. Captain Whitey felt like a tertiary dock. Chucked to the side and stagnant with rot.

33

Captain Whitey was in love. This annoyed him. He had work to do. And his fucking crew. He practiced knots, waiting. His bowline became impeccable. So too his clove hitch. The sheet bend was giving him trouble when Finch flew in frantically. He was screaming in a high voice that Captain Whitey was having trouble understanding. He was also flying around in tight circles so his voice had a weird Doppler effect. He kept saying over and over:

"SBT! SBT!"

"Finch, calm down, I prithee thee!"

"SBT! SBT!"

"Calm down! That's an order!" Finch stopped circling and landed on the ground. He wobbled.

"Oh, dizzy." He threw up.

"Oh Jesus, talk to me, man! Have you news? Where are the men?"

"Moiler!" Finch threw up again. "I must lay down."

"Talk to me damn it! What's SBT?" Finch was using his wings to hold himself up. He looked like he was about to do a push up, but then he collapsed to the ground, and rubbed his eyes with the tips of his wings.

"Screwed, blued and tattooed. Moiler enlisted! He joined the Navy!"

"What are you talking about? How!"

"We were all getting drunk over by the Navy Yard and fucking Moiler joined! He told me to tell you to suck hemp and your victuals are nothing but hardtack and meat meal. His words not mine!"

"That mutinous cunt! When's he set sail?"

"Dawn."

"Haul ass! If we push off now we can cut him by dusk. You're a true mate, Finch. A doubloon for your loyalty." Captain Whitey threw Finch a hunk of bread. He gathered his things quickly and pushed off. He saw Runa washing her ass in the canal as he was leaving the park. His dick became erect and he almost went over and took her to brown

89

town, but he couldn't, and he didn't know if she liked it in the ass anyway. Love would have to wait.

The travel from Park Slope to the Navy Yard felt like a race. They would catch Moiler before he got on that ship come hell or high water. This phrase was stuck in Captain Whitey's mind. Hell or high water. He had heard it once before, but he didn't know what it meant. Hell or high water. Hell or high water.

The underpass of the BQE gave them difficulty. They had to wait for a traffic light twice. Captain Whitey was so impatient that he had to kick something. He was hoping somebody would come by so he could kick their leg. Instead he just kicked a fire hydrant. This didn't help. He spun the metal cross on top. This helped a little. Finch was also acting like a bird, flying back and forth, wondering why it was taking so long. This annoyed Captain Whitey. He said:

"Just go. I know where we're going. I'll be there when I get there. Tell Doctor Sunshine where to find me."

"Yes, sir, I will, sir." Finch flew away.

When Captain Whitey reached the edge of the Navy Yard he sighed in relief. He was sweating and indignant. How could Moiler defect? Meat meal? I'll put you in a meat mill. I serve you filet mignon, and you call it meat meal! But then Captain Whitey remembered a joke he heard when he was in the orphanage while washing dishes:

"Why was the boring flamboyant gay dishwasher like a piece of fancy meat?"

"Because he was a flaming yawn."

Captain Whitey had to stop because he was laughing. Those fuckers, he thought, at least they had good jokes.

Captain Whitey collected himself and hauled ass. A few moments later Doctor Sunshine flew up and landed on the mail cart. Drunk and smoking a cigar. He laughed for a second and then fell into one of the bags. A moment later his cigar burned a hole and fell to the ground. Another moment passed and Captain Whitey could hear snoring. He shook his head. Fucking birds. He would see what he saw when he got where he went, he decided. Doctor Sunshine could sleep it off for all he cared. He just didn't want Moiler to get on that ship.

35

It took another ten minutes for Captain Whitey to get to the port. There was a guard at the entrance. Captain Whitey waited for him to turn his back and then hauled ass in. It was dusk. He went unnoticed. The Navy Yard was vast and open. Ships were moored. Activity was abounding. Giant lengths of rope hung tied to the port. Jovial yells made the action eruptive. Captain Whitey felt at home. It wasn't long before he snuck around the corner of a brick building to find his crew dancing around a fire and smoking and drinking. Moiler included. He approached with a tender stride, not wanting to scare anyone off. His appearance was noted and welcomed. Detective Rabbi and Bunker yelled, "Cappy! You old salt! When'd you get here?" in unison. Then they laughed at each other and hugged.

"Goddamn, you dry mutton chops! Give me a slug!" Captain Whitey was handed a beer. He sat down next to the fire. Smiling. He looked at Moiler, who was swaying and poking at the air with his wing. Captain Whitey said:

"Moiler, cheers, you can't go, we need you."

"Too late, I consigned. Screwed, blued and tattooed."

"Fuck that, there papers?"

"Beans."

"What beans?"

"Your meat is beans, the Navy is gravy."

"You're drunk, man, sleep it off, you'll feel better tomorrow."

"Yeah, I will, when I get on that ship, steaks all night and a guaranteed nap… none of this all day long parlay! You're a rascal, a damn dirty rascal!" Moiler fell over. He punched the air. Then he fell asleep. He was snoring when Captain Whitey picked him up and put him in the same bag that Doctor Sunshine was sleeping in. The rest of birds laughed and then felt tired. They jumped into the the other side of the mail cart and fell asleep. Captain Whitey sighed. He shook his head. He didn't envy the hangover his crew would have in the morning. But he was also glad that Moiler was still with him. He could fly away and get on the ship in the morning, but Captain Whitey knew he wouldn't. His crew was still in tact. It would be a long walk home, but it was worth it, for Moiler. Nobody does it like Maybellene.

36

The walk home was uneventful. The birds snoozed, snored in fact. They talked in their sleep and farted. Captain Whitey felt like he was pushing a cart of delinquent rats that had gotten into the bottom of a rye sack that had been fermenting. They rolled around and made curses on each other. Only waking long enough to spit foul anger at each other. It was comical. He was tired too. He made it to the housing project on Flushing Avenue and Navy Street. He found some open grass and set up camp.

It took some doing to not wake everyone up as he took the newspapers from the mail cart. The birds, though, just rolled and stacked on top of each other in the bottom of the bags. Snoring and farting and talking in their sleep. He laid the newspapers down on the grass. He laid himself down. He covered himself in newspapers. He was very tired. He was asleep before he closed his eyes.

The morning shade was cold. The housing project was tall and towards the east. Six high-rises. Captain Whitey had a dirt clod under his shoulder blade. The dew made the newspaper papers sag. He was waiting for sunlight that never came. There is nothing worse than wet newspaper, he thought as he woke up. The birds were already awake and sitting around a fire drinking coffee, hungover. Captain Whitey felt hungover himself. But not because he was hungover, just because he was tired.

He threw off his newspaper covers and stood up. Hopefully the sun would shine. He doubted it. He would need new covers by night fall. This put him in a rough mood. He became cranky. What next? Doctor Sunshine gets a girlfriend? This thought annoyed him so much that he forced himself to stop thinking it. He went over to a lamp post and took a leak.

The men were all just staring at their coffees not speaking to each other when Captain Whitey showed up at the fire. He sat down next to Moiler and poured himself a cup of coffee. He sat cross-legged. Silent.

After two sips he became animated. He turned to his right, where Moiler was, and said:

"Give it."

"Give what, sir?"

"The tattoo. Show it."

"Ain't nothing, just an anchor."

"Don't care, stick it out."

"Fine, see." Moiler lifted his feathers and showed Captain Whitey the tattoo.

"Fucking hell. I should try you for treason, hang your ass."

"I was drunk, sir."

"We are all drunk, but who the fuck joins the Navy?"

"I was drunk, sir, cut me some slack."

"Yeah, well, you don't seem so broken up about it. I should shove you in the galley, you impetuous roustabout!"

"What do you mean?"

"You know what I mean."

"I don't, sir."

"Yeah, well, think on it." Captain Whitey stood up. He was pissed off. He felt betrayed. He wanted an apple. His teeth felt dirty. He saw some guys playing basketball. He thought about joining the game. But then he remembered he wasn't any good at basketball. He sat down next to his mail cart hoping the sun would come out. The sun never came out. He fell asleep. An hour would pass before he woke up.

37

An hour later Captain Whitey woke up. He felt bad for being so mean to Moiler. He wasn't any less pissed though. The crew needed to parlay, and soon, or else they would be bankrupt. He stood up. The crew was still sitting around smoking and drinking coffee. Finch was mending his sweater. He made a weird noise periodically because he kept poking himself with the needle. Bunker was blathering and Detective Rabbi and Doctor Sunshine were sitting with their heads hung low puffing on their pipes. Beeper was minding his own business. Moiler was nowhere to be seen. The mood felt forced. Captain Whitey understood his men were mad at him for being mad at Moiler. But he was mad at Moiler. He needed loyalty if they had any chance to parlay. That was a fact. A fact that would decide the fate of the crew. He stood up. He needed to be alone. To be solo. A man of his own device. A leader. A leader of men.

38

Captain Whitey walked away from the camp. His heart was heavy. He left his mail cart behind. He knew his men would guard it even if they hated his guts at the moment. The smell of lilacs made him change the route that he had in his mind. It was a smell he found unpleasing. He took a left when normally he would have taken a right. Four blocks later he was standing next to a bridge. He stopped and looked down at the canal. A greasy slime drifted by. A rainbow of grodiness. He smiled. Normally he would just walk with his head down and as fast as he could, but today he was introspective. He was lost in thought when Princess Toots landed on his shoulder. She farted. He shook her off and scrunched his eyes. She flew up and landed on the railing. He glared at her. She blushed. He said:

"What the hell Toots, you can't just fart in a guy's face like that, it's just rude. I'm not in the mood."

"Sorry, Whitey, I can't help it." She bowed her neck. Captain Whitey felt bad.

"Sorry, Toots, just having a bad day. Don't mean to take it out on you. You doing? Where's Runa?"

"No, that's why I'm here. She's under the bridge, she wants you to come down."

"But?"

"Says she smelled you coming." Whitey sighed. Love was painful. He just wanted to parlay. But something tugged him down below. He said:

"Lead the way."

39

Princess Toots flew down under the bridge. Captain Whitey had to take the trail. The canal smelled like moss and dirt-mud. It felt wet and grassy and rocky. There was a cropping that Runa had splayed her bedding on. She was naked and fingering her clitoris. Maybellene was pecking at her pussy lips. Shortly thereafter, Princess Toots was too. Runa spread her legs. She moaned in pleasure. Her hair looked like a squirrel trying to run away from her head. Captain Whitey was stunned. He stood there with a hard-on. His dick was so hard that he had to whack it against the concrete pillar just to prove it existed. Runa said:

"Take off your pants." Captain Whitey took his pants off. His shirt too. He literally whacked his dick against the concrete pillar and said:

"Ding, dong."

The two birds flew up to Runa's nipples and started pecking. Captain Whitey went over and kneeled down. His plan was to lick her private parts, but his penis was too hard and too exposed. He couldn't help himself. He buried his dick in her vagina. The birds pecked at her nipples. The smell was awful. The canal, and the homeless pirate Captain Whitey, and the homeless Runa, it was a rapture of old socks and dirty buttholes. And then the birds. Princess Toots farting the whole time, and Maybellene smacking him in the face with her wing. Nobody cared though. Runa came fast and hard. Squirting. This made Captain Whitey come too. He pulled out. The come knocked Princess Toots and Maybellene over and sprayed over Runa's shoulder. They all collapsed into a heap of stinking ass, come and bird farts, combined with dick and cunt and canal. Runa and Captain Whitey had smiles on their faces. The birds had beaks, but were satisfied. Captain Whitey dug his head into the dirt that was next to Runa's neck and said:

"Goddamn."

40

Captain Whitey woke up alone under the bridge. Clods of dirt stuck to his belly. His mouth was crusted with dirt as well. It took him a moment to open his eyes. His pants were over there, he thought. His dick was deep in the dirt. He was hard. His dick made a popping noise as he rolled over. The sunshine was everywhere else but under the bridge. He felt cool. He waited for his hard-on to dissipate. The wet dirt on his ass made things sensual. His boner refused to go away. He laid there frustrated. All the smells of the foursome were still lingering. He couldn't help himself. He looked around. He didn't care. He just wanted to know if he had an audience. Nobody lurked.

His hand was sandy as he touched his boner. It felt like sandpaper as he started to stroke. Barely twenty seconds went by before he ejaculated. A pebble that was lodged in the tip of his dick came barreling out. It whizzed past his ear and twanged against one of the metal pillars that held the bridge up. He heard it splash into the canal. He suddenly felt self-aware. He grabbed his pants and put them on. Come dribbled down the front. The dirt caked on the underside of his dick scraped off as he pulled his pants up. His pants were still buttoned. This created a clod that fell to the ground. The head of his dick got stuck and he had to push it down. When his dick entered his pants it swung down and whacked his balls and sand fell down his pant legs. The sensation was unsettling. He wanted to take his pants back off and shake them out, but he had a sense of urgency that he couldn't explain. He needed to run away. He ran away without thinking.

Two blocks later he was aware again. He was holding his shoes in one hand and scratching his face with the other. Chunks of dirt were falling off. His stomach itched. He scratched it. Clods of dirt fell to the ground. He sat down on the sidewalk and put his shoes on. A greasy dog shit sat coiled in the gutter next to his feet. A cockroach ran by, nose to the grindstone. This hurt Captain Whitey's feelings. He needed to parlay more than anything, but he just kept getting distracted. And now the cockroaches won't even stop and talk. The dog shit was greasy enough that he could at least laugh at it. It looked like the result of a bacon diet. That is too much bacon for a dog, he was thinking, when Maybellene landed next to him. He brushed her away. She flew up and landed again. He got frustrated and crossed his arms. He said:

"Where'd you guys go? I got sick with worry." He was being sarcastic.

"Runa sent a note." Maybellene was bobbing and cooing. She didn't care about the dog shit.

"A note from her tuba I suppose, her song's a little flat, can't say I am waiting for the refrain."

"She loves you, Captain Whitey."

"Yeah? I love a good piece of toast, doesn't mean I ask a meter maid for a quarter stick of butter."

"She thought you might say that, she said I should give you this."

Maybellene unzipped Captain Whitey's pants. It happened so quickly that he didn't even really register. He was so oversexed that it came naturally. His dick was erect. The next thing he knew he was getting a hand job from a bird. The feathers were soft and silky. She was looking up at him, her beak straight, her eyes vacant. Captain Whitey enjoyed it for a second, and he then panicked. He shooed her away. He was suddenly ashamed. Love was making him do stupid things. He needed to parlay. Just parlay, just once. That was the answer!

Maybellene flew back down and tried to grab onto him again.

Captain Whitey stood up and ran away while zipping his pants, yelling:

"Parlay! Parlay!"

Captain Whitey was running down the street yelling "parlay" over and over again. His postal uniform was a mess at this point. There was dirt caked to most of it, and the cuffs on both the ankles and the wrists were black.

He was met by Finch two blocks down. Finch joined in with the mantra:

"Parlay! Parlay!"

They ran back to camp. Captain Whitey found this hilarious. He spun around a couple times during the run, kicking over trash cans. By the time they got back to camp they were both exhausted and dizzy. Finch landed by the fire the crew had built and threw up. Captain Whitey did an Egyptian dance and then threw up himself. First getting down on all fours, his hands and knees, and then collapsing next to the pile of vomit, out of breath and gasping.

The men all laughed. Spirits got high. Detective Rabbi lit his pipe and bellowed:

"A pox on your scurvy junker, lubber!" The men all laughed again. Moments later the rum appeared. Soon thereafter the crew was drunk, Captain Whitey included.

43

The crew was back to normal. All ill will was gone. Because they were men, there was nothing to talk about. They drank rum and told stories. Near the end of the night, as the fire became coals, someone asked Captain Whitey what he had been doing all day. It was Doctor Sunshine, and he was curious about the Captain. The rest of the crew was too, but they were scared to ask. It took a moment for Captain Whitey to respond. He had to think about it. The day was a burner, he decided, a day meant to be lost, he would equate it to a vacation, but he had never taken a vacation, he only knew about things that disintegrate. Like fire and wood.

A moment went by. The silence was offset by the sound of popping coals. The mood was as heavy as a sandbag. Finally, with levity, he said:

"I understand love now, my friends." The birds gasped. They did not expect such a heavy response. The statement had the opposite effect of being jovial. A sadness fell, like a dead pine tree falling into a creek, the cold green needles still clinging to the branches as the brown ones floated away. The roots still trying to grab the earth. The silent violence of death. Captain Whitey went on:

"Love is a boner." Captain Whitey's eyes became black and reflected the red and black coals."It's hard at first, so hard you can't control it, and then it works its way into a frenzy, a frenzy no man can explain, the earth moves underneath you, the stars lub and lub alike, a pox on all shores, aft to fore, privy to hardtack, all corners of the drink, avast. Avast! From shaft to tip a man can think of nothing else! And the glory that gang's way, the mist on the fabled albatross disappears into the salty mist. And thee, thee in thine own mind, makes murder of sirens bashing their fists on the stones of port, wishing for a single strand of hair to tie to their lover's heart, just to keep him safe, a sliver from a barrel, just to keep him aloft for one more second more, before the depths reclaim him, and leave she barren on the rocky nips pulling on that string. That lure, that holds his heart afloat. Yes, love is a boner, a merciless boner." Captain Whitey was looking at the stars now. His hand under his chin.

"Fuck that!" Professor Rabbi said. "Finch said you were doing it."

"Oh! I was! It was great! I humped Runa and her birds! We should have a party and invite them over!"

The crew erupted in excitement. A party was a great way to begin a parlay. And there would be women involved. As drunk as they were they all started to plan on how to clean up. Doctor Sunshine was going to cut his hair. Moiler was planning to shave his beak. Finch was going to get a breath mint. They all decided to clean the camp up in the morning. Professor Rabbi was thinking of trimming down below. Beeper was going to pierce his ears and get two golden hoops "for the ladies." Bunker didn't know what to do, so he decided he would make a sign that said:

"Party Hardy, Don't Be Tardy."

44

The next morning didn't work as well as everybody thought it would. The hangovers were severe. Moiler was the first to wake up. He'd slept on a rock so his side hurt. His neck was cricked. His mouth was dry and his eyes barely opened. He rolled around for a moment groaning. He stood up and immediately puked. He stumbled over to the canal and took a long, greasy swallow. He puked again and sat down. Roosting. The cold dirt felt nice on his underside. The sound of water splashing against the shore was calming. The day was hot already. He tucked his head under his wing and went back to sleep. The sun beat down like a dribbling basketball. Loud and high-pitched. Painful and disruptive.

Captain Whitey woke next. He stood up and pissed in the bushes. He felt stupid but happy. Pissing made him thirsty. He went to the water fountain. Moving his lips to drink made his lips crack and bleed. The water tasted like batteries. His forehead was sweating. He found some shade under a tree and laid down. He went back to sleep.

Moiler and Finch woke up next. They were sleeping in each other's arms, wings. Moiler yawned. His breath was like a hand grenade made of dog shit. Finch smelled it and flew away ASAP. He landed on Captain Whitey's head. The shade felt nice. He snuggled himself in Captain Whitey's hair and fell asleep. Moiler bobbed around for a moment before flying over to Captain Whitey. He landed on his legs. Captain Whitey, still sleeping, put his hand on him. Moiler cooed and fell back to sleep.

Bunker didn't wake up, but was talking in his sleep. This woke both Detective Rabbi and Doctor Sunshine. They were only slightly hungover. They built a fire. They stared at the fire in silence until the wood became coals. Soon after, the coffee was percolating. Soon after that they were holding cups of steaming coffee. Detective Rabbi broke the silence. He said:

"The funny thing about haircuts is that you gotta keep getting them, ya know? I mean, they're a goddamned time ghost, not so sure it's the way to go."

"Yeah, right? They make me nervous. I mean, nobody asked me my opinion, ya know? I don't want to look at that."

"Don't do it then."

"Yeah, but the ladies."

"Let me tell you about the ladies, the ladies like the big muscles, they like the fat wallet and the Machu Picchu ding-a-ling. You want my two cents, get stronger."

"But I can't get any stronger."

"Invest in worm futures then."

Detective Rabbi and Doctor Sunshine returned to silence. The coffee ran out. They both flew off in different directions looking for ground to peck on. Moiler woke up and flew off himself. Bunker woke up confused that nobody was around. He pecked at his feathers for a second, said about a hundred words, then said, "Beans, beans, beans," then flew away.

Finch stirred and shit on Captain Whitey's face. This woke him up. He said, "Goddammit!" and shooed Finch away. He rubbed the shit off his face and stood up. The heat was black. The canal smelled like a diaper filled with diarrhea. The city felt like a sweaty baby that was too hot to nap. Irritable and screaming. Captain Whitey shook his head. His hands tingled with sweat. In the distance a boat blew its horn. He remembered the parlay, and the party they were supposed to throw. His mood changed. He thought about Runa. He decided he should get a party sub. Nothing sweeter than a juicy, meaty sandwich for a party of all effects, he thought. But how? He thought he might know how. He got his cart and pushed off. A slight breeze kicked in. Pleasant beginnings.

45

The streets were filled with angry, smelly jerks. Everywhere Captain Whitey turned he was met with disdain. Plastic cups filled with ice and the remnants of milk and sugar were thrown at him at every trash can he visited. Nobody was nice to him. He didn't care. He collected the ice in a deli bag for the party. Before long the bag was filled. He poked a hole in the bottom so the liquid would drain out. The ice was brown with coffee. He put it in the mail cart hoping it would last until nightfall. He held onto the cups as well. When he had enough for everybody he stopped collecting more. He put these on top of the ice. He stopped thinking of drinks and turned instead to the problem of the party sub.

The meats he found were unpleasant but fine. He had smelled worse. Had eaten worse. He thought for certain they would stay okay if he just put them on top of the ice under the cups. He was lucky in meat. The three delis that he knew of, that discarded their yesterday's meats in the morning, all did so on the same day. Now all he needed was bread.

He was lucky in bread as well. The bread factory's trash had a full bag of half-moldy bread he could parlay without a single bad word from the owners. He took the bag and ran back to camp. He spent an hour breaking off hunks and making sandwiches. The moldy pieces made a pile next to him. Their fate, to rot. He placed the sandwiches in his mail cart, on top of the ice. Feeling tired, he found a piece of shade and laid down. Things would be fine, he thought, and drifted off to sleep.

The smell of fire woke Captain Whitey up. All the birds were sitting around it talking. Dusk was upon them. Captain Whitey was startled. He slept too long, of course, but he also realized that he never told Runa and her birds about the party. He ran in a panic to the campfire yelling:

"We never told them bitches! Them bitches!"

"'Lax dog, we got you covered, Bunker's been running PR." Detective Rabbi was smoking his pipe. His eyes smiled.

"But when?"

"As you slept. They'll be here in an hour."

"Runa too?!"

"Of course, sandwiches?"

"Mail cart." They all looked over at the mail cart standing limp underneath the tree. Its side was dark and water was dripping from the bottom. "Or, I guess."

Captain Whitey walked over to the mail cart and opened the flap. There was a soup of soggy bread and slimy sliced meats. He hung his head and sighed. His big idea became flaccid. He put his hand into the soup. There was still a few ice cubes and the water was cold. He pulled out a slice of ham. He smelled it. He frowned. He dumped the cart over. The remains of the sandwiches and the ice spilled onto the ground. A loss. An anti-parlay. But what could be done? He put the cart right again. His men were watching him. Their mouths half opened. The fire playing dances on their beaks. They all had white eyes. Captain Whitey walked over. His grimace was as dark as a seal's wet back. The men shuddered. Only Detective Rabbi had the courage to speak. He said:

"What now, Cappy?" Captain Whitey stood there for a second. He frowned. But a second later he smiled like a cemetery of bleached tombstones and said:

"We drink!"

The men erupted in laughter. The rum came out. Thirty minutes later they were all drunk and wondering where the women were at.

46

The women showed up on accident. Bunker's PR work meant that he flew around for a while and made a bunch of noise. He never saw Runa or Maybellene or Princess Toots. He caught hell when he got back to camp. They all asked him where the women were. He told them he had no idea what they were talking about. They thought he was joking at first, but the more they pressed the less they received. His responses became more and more vague until Captain Whitey asked him directly, "Where have you been for the last hour?"

"Oh! You know what I mean? I mean, I mean, I had a good, nice time, ya dig, there's this guy over by the park, by that place where the times you get chased, um, the thing where the little guys like to try to grab you, you know, know what I mean, the little ones?"

"Kids?"

"Yeah, the kids, the ones that chase you, you know what I mean? Where the kids are, the park."

"Yes, Bunker, the kids, but what park?"

"What do you mean? I mean the park, with the kids, you know what I mean? The park where they chase you."

"But what about Runa and her friends? Did you see them?"

"Oh! Of course I saw them, they were by the park."

"Did you talk to them?"

"Them? Of course not! They were doing something, no, I was with this guy, you know this guy? That's my point, don't you remember my point?" Captain Whitey shrugged and decided to let Bunker just get it out. He said:

"I forgot your point, Bunker, sock it to me."

"What do you mean? Socks, ha! Can you imagine wearing socks? I don't like socks, they get stuck on my nails. Nails are sharp, you ever notice that?"

"The guy, tell us about the guy."

"What guy? The guy wearing socks? I don't remember a guy wearing socks. I guess I could wear some socks if I just curled my toes, you know what I mean? About the socks, I mean. What are you guys doing? Where are the women at?" Bunker looked around. The men were staring at him with careful dark faces. He bobbed his head and picked at his chest. He said:

"Ok, let me know when the women get here, I'm gonna go find this sock guy, he sounds nice." He flew away. Captain Whitey shook his head. The men went back to getting drunk.

47

An hour later the men were arm-wrestling. A bonfire was burning. Captain Whitey was staring at the stars and pontificating. H e was leaning on a log and talking to Doctor Sunshine, who was glassy-eyed and loading a pipe. He offered it to Captain Whitey, who said, "No thanks," and "Maybe later." Doctor Sunshine shrugged and lit the pipe. Captain Whitey spoke. He said:

"Sometimes I hope the stars ain't stars, because they make me feel alone. Makes me feel stupid, like I am just as stupid as they are. Know what I mean? I mean, if I am just the same as them, then I am just as stupid as them, like I am a star myself, and can see them the same way they see me. Just saying that makes me feel stupid, shit, talk to me, Sunshine."

"The women!" Doctor Sunshine yelled. They both sat up. The women randomly showed up. Runa appeared by the bonfire with Maybellene and Princess Toots on her shoulders. Her bird-shit covered poncho was lit up. It looked hieroglyphic in flame light. Her hair seemed tangled and dancing. The redness was moving like a hypnotic snake. Her face was perched in a profound awareness. Her birds were erect as sphinxes on her shoulders. Magic exploded upon the scene. The men stopped the arm-wrestling. They sat with their beaks open. Captain Whitey stood up. His eyes were open, but the rest of his knowledge took a full minute to catch up to where his body was. He squeaked out a noise. "Runa." Another moment went by. She said:

"I heard there was a party, this shit's a stinker, what the fuck?" Captain Whitey shook his head. Enough defensive thoughts destroyed his insecurities that he said:

"Who the hell told you that?"

"Some guy at the park where the little guys chase the birds, ever hear of it?"

"Fucking Bunker, I suppose." The men put their pipes and cigars down. They preened their feathers. Bobbed their heads. Hid their rum. Waxed their beaks.

"Who's Bunker?"

"He's a guy, but I mean, there is a party, you guys down?"

"We're here, ain't we?" Runa made a face that was half-smile, half-sneer. The birds on her shoulders flew to the ground next to the men. She walked over to Captain Whitey and slapped him in the crotch. He bent over because of the pain in his balls. She said:

"Don't fuck with me."

48

The party started in earnest. When Captain Whitey recovered from being slapped in the balls he tackled Runa and they rolled into the bushes. Her curly red locks getting snagged on the branches. She punched him in the face a couple times. Laughed, then took his boner inside of herself. The interaction was over in minutes. They came together. Captain Whitey had a mouthful of dirt. He spit it out as he rolled over staring at the stars again and breathing hard. Runa fell asleep immediately. She was snoring and farting. Captain Whitey smiled and stroked her hair. He couldn't sleep so he stood up to join the men. Runa rolled over and hugged a branch. She let a big one loose. Captain Whitey shook his head and smiled. She was an angel. An angel snagged by her curly red hair lying in the detritus of a flowering bush. She looked like a china doll being dragged into the bush by murderous squirrels. Her legs spread. Come dripping down her thighs. A puffy shock of rusty pubes leading to a slice of pink bacon. Captain Whitey almost woke her up to make love again. He decided to let her sleep.

49

The bonfire was blaring when Captain Whitey joined the party. Detective Rabbi and Moiler were jumping over it trying to impress the ladies. Beeper was puking in the bushes and yelling, "Parlay, bitches!" Bunker had returned. He had Princess Toots cornered and was going off about some nonsense. She looked bored. Maybellene was chugging rum and yelling at Detective Rabbi and Moiler, telling them they were a bunch of pussies. Finch was slightly stunned. He wasn't sure if he should join in, or boil some water and read the Bible. Doctor Sunshine was smoking a pipe and sipping on rum, bemused. When Captain Whitey sat down next to him, he said:

"We got quite the crew." He tamped out his pipe and loaded it again. He lit it. "Drop an anchor?"

"Dropped it abysmal, Davy Jones style. That girl reeks for weeks, twists my wick, think I'm in love."

"I noticed. Careful, she'll lub ya yet."

"Don't worry about me, I'll parlay all you bitches before the dawn makes pancakes, hand me that rum!" Captain Whitey took a huge drink. He spit on the ground. Moiler fell into the fire and burned a serious amount of feathers off. Everybody laughed. He rolled around for a while and then ran into the canal to cool off. Princess Toots took this opportunity to get away from Bunker and sat down next to Detective Rabbi who had stopped jumping over the fire but had somehow taken the fire into his eyes. After a minute they both disappeared into the bushes. Bunker didn't understand and flew away. Finch couldn't take anymore himself. He flew off to either masturbate or read the Bible. Beeper was face down in his own puke, snoring. Doctor Sunshine and Captain Whitey sat in silence. The fire burned down. They drank rum. Doctor Sunshine smoked. Runa snored and farted. The stars mocked them. Maybellene, who had been sitting just on the periphery, bobbed over without a word and held out her wing to Doctor Sunshine. He handed his pipe to Captain Whitey. His boner was visible by the fire light. They disappeared into the bushes.

Captain Whitey sat next to the dying fire listening to his men have sex in the bushes. Listening to his love snore and flatulate, drinking rum and holding his first mate's pipe.

When he stood up to piss, nearly an hour later, he could barely stand up. All the birds were snoring now. Bunker and Finch had returned. He put Doctor Sunshine's pipe in his pocket and walked over to Runa. He pissed near her feet. He then stumbled and collapsed into the bushes next to her. His pants down. She didn't wake up. He was passed out before he could apologize.

50

The morning smelled like hot-dogs and headache. Only Runa wasn't hungover. She started tugging on Captain Whitey's dick. He was so sensitive that he came on accident. The come was hot and wet, like a cup of tea being poured on his stomach. Runa giggled and kissed him on the cheek. She gathered her things and left. Captain Whitey laid there with his eyes half open watching the clouds drift past. His back was being stabbed by branches so he rolled over. He pulled his pants up. His face was smashed into leaves. The smell of Runa's hair was still there. He went back to sleep.

Later, when he opened his eyes, he could hear his men making breakfast. He stood up and buttoned his pants. The zipper caught his pubes. He let out a little shriek and pulled the zipper back down again. When he pulled it back up again he was successful. He tucked his shirt in and went to the campfire. None of the girl birds were there. Just the men. They were lively and in good spirits. They were cooking bacon and pancakes. And coffee. The cup of coffee he was offered was exactly what he needed. He sat with it steaming on his face for long enough that is was almost cold when he took his first drink. The men bobbed around making breakfast without saying much to each other. Before long he had a hot plate of bacon and pancakes in front of him. He realized his men were waiting for orders. They wanted nothing more than to parlay. He silently ate his victuals. The rock by his foot started talking to him. "Now or never" were its only words. Now or never. Captain Whitey finished his breakfast. He handed his plate to Bunker. He said:

"The rock says 'Now or never.' Today, we parlay!"

The men were so excited they flew away, leaving Captain Whitey to clean up camp. He grumbled:

"Always a bridesmaid," he said, as he went about the homework.

51

Captain Whitey cleaned up camp. He made right his mail cart. The remnants of the sandwich idea sat steaming in a pile. The sun slapped down on him like he was a hamburger on somebody's backyard grill. He sizzled and crusted. There was nothing he could avoid, so he double-checked that his camp was correct and pushed off into the sweltering void.

He needed more hardtack. Water. Victuals. The first deposit he came to only had a bag of dog shit and an empty package of cigarettes. He took the paper out of the package of cigarettes. He left the bag of dog shit. The next deposit he came to was outside of a barber shop. He found a bag of hair. He put the hair in his mail cart. There was also a half-eaten piece of pizza with pepperoni on it. He ate this casually as he pushed down the street, pausing every now and again to remove a hair or two from his mouth. A few blocks later he found a deposit that was a sweatband for his wrist. It was white and soiled. He put this on. His arm felt cooler. He smiled and allowed himself to sweat a little bit more, but just on his right arm. The next few deposits yielded nothing. He got too hot to move around anymore. He stopped under a tree and sat down in the shade. The few blades of grass struggling for life made the dirt feel welcoming. People stared at him as they walked past but said nothing. They also ignored him deeply. He wished for some water, but instead fell asleep.

Captain Whitey woke because of thunder. The sky was dark, and the air was electric, cool. Huge drops of rain started falling. People were running for cover. He thought about doing the same, but then the wind came up. Suddenly his mail cart was in danger. He held onto it for dear life as the wind tried to blow it away. Rain pelted his body. Dust and debris tore down the street. He thought, "Batten the hatches!" The tree swayed and buckled. Branches broke. A sheet of rain sprang from the sky, dousing him in a way like God himself was coming on his face. He screamed into the wind, "Give me all you got! You scurvy cur!" The wind blew. Branches broke. Lightning struck, then thunder.

He was soaked to the skin. His wristband drenched. Yet still he held tight to the mail cart! Yes, still, he battened his hatches and braced against the storm.

Five minutes later he was sitting in a puddle of dirty water. The storm passed. The mail cart intact. The sun peeking through the clouds like a naughty child laughing about what she had just done. Captain Whitey was drenched, through and through. His dick was rock hard. He sat for a second thinking. He decided there was nothing to do about anything. He stood up. His dick now bulging and apparent. Vulgar. It ran sidewise nearly reaching the outside edge of his left hip. You could see the outline of the head through his thin greasy pants. A woman that had been under the cover of an awning nearby walked past him. She got scandalized and ran away leaving a kind of squeaky noise behind herself. Whether it was a high-pitched fart or a scream, Captain Whitey couldn't tell. He didn't care either.

The sun became a bully again and put Captain Whitey in a headlock. Her knuckles grinding into his scalp. His clothes were still wet, but chafed now instead of soothed. His ass was dirty and annoying. He frowned for a second and limped back home to the camp.

52

The camp was a mess again. The storm had destroyed everything. None of his men had returned. Captain Whitey sighed. He took off all his clothes and draped them on bushes. The sun felt nice on his naked body. He went to the canal and washed his dirty butt in the greasy, stagnant waters. He was thirsty so he went to the drinking fountain. This caused a few shrieks from the caretakers of the small children that were now playing at the playground. Captain Whitey ignored this until he found himself in handcuffs, naked and confused. Men in uniform were yelling at him. He didn't understand. He was just thirsty and wet. He watched the men put his mail cart and uniform in the trunk of a car. The next thing he knew he was in the back seat of the same car. The seats were plastic. The coolness felt nice on his ass. One of the windows was down. Finch flew up. Panic was in his eyes. Captain Whitey said, "Don't worry, Finch, it's all okay. Just tell the guys, you understand? Tell the guys!" Finch looked confused. The window started to roll up. He had to fly away. Captain Whitey kept yelling, "Tell the guys! Tell the guys!" as the police car drove away.

Captain Whitey couldn't tell if Finch understood. It didn't matter now. The handcuffs bit into his hands as the car barreled down the streets, its siren blaring. Something from his past came back to him, but he wasn't sure exactly what. He had a bad feeling. Things, he thought, were about to get worse.

53

Things did get worse. Captain Whitey bounced around in the back of the police car. His naked ass sliding back and forth on the plastic seat. His hands in handcuffs. He kept trying to look out the window to see if anyone was coming to help him, but every time the car took a sharp turn he either whacked his head on the glass or slid to the other side. Then he would try to look out that window, and the same thing would happen again. He was helpless to brace himself. He was small. The physics was bullying. Plus, his hands were in handcuffs.

At one point the car turned so sharp he was thrown onto the floor. The floor was dirty and stuck to his skin. It took him a moment to notice, but his hands were suddenly in front of himself. The handcuffs were off too. He sat back on the seat. He braced himself as the police car sped along. He looked out the window while wiping dirt chunks and debris off his once wet, but now humid naked body. He saw no birds. No birds coming to the rescue. He frowned. He was lost and confused. He had no idea where he was. It looked like Brooklyn. But a different part of Brooklyn than he knew. The birds would know, he thought. His men knew all the parts. Captain Whitey let out a whistle that his men would understand. The policemen in the front whacked on the window that separated them from him. They told him to shut the fuck up if he knew what was good for him. Captain Whitey felt helpless. He held himself in place. The motion eventually made him sick. He puked on the handcuffs. The smell made him move to the other side of the backseat. He looked out the window. Nothing doing. No birds. No men. He was about to puke again when the car came to a halt. Thank god, he thought.

When the police officers opened the door they screamed:

"Holy shit! He's loose!" They pulled out their guns and pointed them at Captain Whitey. Captain Whitey was merely huddled next to the window trying not to puke. He held his hands up. He looked like a child. He was naked. His teeth were exposed because he was trying to hold the puke in. He pulled his knees into his chest. This was taken as an act of aggression. One of the officers yelled:

"Hands up, motherfucker!" Captain Whitey held his hands up. He didn't have the sense to be scared, but he knew better than to ignore the two men. One of them yelled:

"Handcuffs, motherfucker!" Captain Whitey made the mistake of trying to point to where the handcuffs were instead of using words. The next thing he knew his ears were ringing and he was covered in broken glass. "Next one's yours! Next one's yours! Where are the fucking handcuffs?" Whitey was suddenly aware that two policemen were pointing guns at him and one of them had just shot the window above him. He threw his hands back in the air and shit himself. He was shaking and mumbling. "Speak up, you asshole!" Whitey said:

"The puke, under the puke." The policemen both looked down. The handcuffs were indeed covered in puke on the floor. "Well, what the fuck?" one of them said as the other one grabbed him by the leg and dragged him out of the back of the police car. He slid through his own shit and fell to the ground. They both kicked him until there was blood coming out of Whitey's mouth. They spit on him. One of them opened the trunk and got his clothes out. They were still sopping wet and hot now from being in the trunk. He threw them on top of Whitey. He said:

"Put these on."

Whitey did his best to put the clothes on. They were very wet and wadded. His body hurt. The puddle of blood he was in made the friction slippery. The ground.

Suddenly there were five pigeons and a finch bouncing around next to his head. He smiled. He loved birds. He tried to reach out and touch them. One of the policemen kicked them away. He said, "What the fuck's with these birds?" He kicked Whitey in the head. Whatever Whitey had in his head went black.

54

Whitey woke up on a bed. His head hurt. His body hurt. He knew where he was, he didn't like it. There was a tray of iceberg lettuce and pudding and some sort of meat chunk next to him. His clothes felt like soldier cloth, stiff and utilitarian. He groaned and smelled bad smells. Most of them from himself. He rolled over the best he could and grabbed the bunch of lettuce. He just wanted the water. He sucked on the lettuce. The lettuce ran out of juice. He fell asleep chewing on it.

Time went by. He woke up to another tray of food, this time it had macaroni and hot-dogs. He was hungry enough that he sat up and ate it. There was more iceberg lettuce. He saved this until last. He laid down and sucked on it. His body still hurt, but so what, he had been beaten before, his bed felt like a hammock. He squeezed the rest of the water out of the lettuce into his mouth and threw the hunk in his hand on the ground like a lime at some horrible resort. He smiled. He went back to sleep.

The next tray of food had chicken and cream sauce. He was about to eat this when he heard a knock on his window. It was Doctor Sunshine. Whitey got up to look. He had forgotten about Doctor Sunshine. But he suddenly recognized him. He grabbed the bars on the window. He almost started yelling, but Doctor Sunshine put the tip of his wing to his beak, meaning "shush." He pointed with his wing. This made Captain Whitey back away from the wall.

There was huge blast and the room filled with dust.

Captain Whitey could see a huge hole in the wall. Next thing he knew he was running down the street. His men had his mail cart waiting for him on the corner. Detective Rabbi was yelling, "Haul ass!" Bunker was shitting turds like nobody's business. Moiler kept yelling, "I got your back! I got your back!" Finch couldn't take it, he flew away. Beeper was hopping up and down. He had a little bird boner that was making tiny smacking noises against his stomach. A bunch of men came screaming out of the hole in the jail. They were waving black sticks.

Captain Whitey and his men turned a corner and ditched the attackers. They huddled behind a dumpster, out of breath. Moiler said:

"Holy shit!"

"Goddamn! What the hell, dudes?" Captain Whitey said, "You saved my ass!"

The men and Captain Whitey sat there catching their breath. The dumpster smelled like curled oysters and burnt sideburns. The parlay was pretty direct before, but now it was fugitive.

55

They waited for nightfall behind the stinky dumpster. Every noise was an enemy. Every shift in light, a predator. When they thought the coast was clear they crept out into the open. Every feather in tune with the vibrations of the earth. Every eye as sharp as chipped glass. Every ear squeezing the sounds so hard there was wax dripping down earlobes. A cat jumped down from a fence halfway down the block. Somebody panicked and yelled, "Run!" They took off running. The birds flying, Captain Whitey pushing his cart. He couldn't keep up. The birds disappeared. Ten blocks later he felt safe and stopped running. He was sweaty and hot. Captain Whitey sat down on stoop and tried to figure out where he was. There were none of the normal indications to identify with. No clock tower. No river. No canal. Only brownstones. He must be north, he decided. He looked at the stars in the sky. He tried to remember if he had learned to navigate by the stars. The answer was no. He knew what a sextant was, but he didn't have one, and even if he did, he wouldn't know how to use it. All his sea knowledge had came from a book, or more specifically, a pamphlet called "The Captain's Specific Orders," which he had read at one point in his life. He couldn't remember when. Or where. Or how he had acquired the thing. He was lost, adrift. He decided to make himself comfortable and wait for the dawn. But then what, he thought as he curled himself into a ball on the steps of an unknown brownstone in a part of town that was peaceful and serene. He closed his eyes. A moment later he was asleep. Dreaming of parlay.

56

The morning came with a scream and a broom. A young pretty white woman was banging on the steps and yelling. She was too scared to actually come down the steps, but held the broom like a weapon, she would whack him, she said, if he didn't get going, get gone, get out. If not, she would call the cops. Captain Whitey was confused, he had been so sweetly asleep, but he didn't want to get whacked with a broom, and he didn't want her to call the cops. He got up and pushed the mail cart away. He looked back for some reason. She had a face like a boiled asshole, puckered and finished. She shook the broom again. She wore a nightgown and in her violent actions her breasts had been exposed. They were huge and quite beautiful. Captain Whitey stared for a second until she got scared again and threw the broom in his direction. It hit a fence and made a twang sound. Then fell hollow to the ground. The look on Captain Whitey's face made her look down. She noticed her breasts were exposed. She called him a pervert and stormed back inside slamming the door. Captain Whitey shrugged. He wanted nothing to do with her huge tits and her broom, and even more than that, her stoop was a stinker.

57

Captain Whitey finally knew where west was. Or east, or whatever. The sun was out. He headed back to the park. What he couldn't understand though was where his men had gotten the explosives to blow the wall open. This thought sent him onto a rhythm of introspection. He hardly noticed the path he was taking. He needed to go west, that was all. He would get there eventually. He pushed past brownstone after brownstone. Then fast-moving traffic. Then ghetto. Then brownstone and brownstone. Then even faster moving traffic. He was lost in thought though. His thoughts went like this:

"That's not dynamite, that's daylight. I mean, who does that? I mean, those jerks could barely knock a dingleberry from a dead goat's scrotum covered in ants, in honey bees and handshakes! Parlay? Ha! I'd like to see that! But blow a hole in the wall? What's that? Mercenary? Should I be scared? Do my men know something I don't know? I don't know, I don't know, I mean, I don't know. I'd like to see that. Know what I mean? I'd like to see that."

Captain Whitey had a paranoia, but he was also still reeling from his time in the clink. He felt like he knew something he wasn't certain of. The word felt kept coming to his mind. Felt. Felt. Kept felt. Something kept felt, kept coming. Something he was feeling kept coming. He hoped it was parlay. Parlay was good, parlay was a nice thing. He would like a parlay. He felt a nice parlay coming his direction would be a good thing. Captain Whitey returned to the world a block and a half from his camp by the canal. He hadn't solved the explosives rift, but he didn't care, he would just ask Doctor Sunshine.

58

When Captain Whitey walked into camp his men were sitting around a fire. They were half-cocked on rum and Finch was back. They were cooking hot-dogs on a stick. Each one was biting the tip off when it got hot enough to eat. They all looked up and smiled with their beaks as Captain Whitey pushed the cart next them and sat down. Words were unnecessary. Captain Whitey found a stick. He took out his knife. He whittled the tip down to a point. He shoved the stick into one of the hot-dogs. He put it into the fire. The tip buckled and burst. A blister of flavor. He bit the tip off while blowing quick breaths as it cooled on his tongue. He did this again two more times. When he was done he sucked on the stick. When he was done sucking on the stick he threw it into the fire. The fire flamed up, then died back down. Captain Whitey stared at Doctor Sunshine for a moment. He was sitting on the other side of the fire. Doctor Sunshine became self-conscious and put his head under his wing. Captain Whitey said:

"Don't be weird guys, everything is cool, we can still parlay. We just had a momentary setback. What's the big wow?"

"I don't...." Moiler suddenly got self-conscious and put his head under his wing.

"You don't what? Understand why I went to jail? That's nothing. Not now, not ever. We are free and clear. Understand? Fuck them bitches, come get us, I dare them."

"Yeah, but we are fugitives now. They are going to be looking out." Detective Rabbi hid his head right after saying this. Shaking.

"Ah, fuck! Come on guys, you blew the doors off a prison! I think we can still parlay! All we really need to do is to focus, know what I mean? Not only that, but where the hell did you get the explosive? Moiler, you? Detective Rabbi? Doctor Sunshine? Bunker?"

"It was Finch, sir," Doctor Sunshine said as he pulled his head out from behind his wing. "He knows a guy." Finch twitched with pride, then flew away with embarrassment. All the men chuckled. "He hooked us up."

139

"Well, goddamn! What a sweetheart! Who?"

"That stupid stork, you know him, Daddy Long Legs, we had to give him all the victuals we had. We are back to zero, boss. The parlay is stalled." Doctor Sunshine's eyes became sad.

"Yeah, I think not, the parlay is greater than ever! That fucker can suck it. I say we raid him tomorrow, make death where his memories should be! Make him eat lead like the sweet-tooth he is! What do you say, boys! Parlay?!"

The men erupted with excitement. The smell of war broke like water from the corpulence of death giving birth to a whetstone. I will only sharpen your resolve. You fat motherfucker.

59

The rest of the evening descended into excitement. The men drank and planned. Captain Whitey made a map out of twigs and dirt clods. Daddy Long Legs' camp was on the base of a hill, they would attack from the top of that hill. They prepared their weapons. Prepared themselves for war, for death. By midnight the men were ready. They all drank as much water as they possibly could. This was their alarm clock. They would sleep until they had to get up to piss. At most, three hours from then. This would give them plenty of time to sneak onto the top of the hill and get themselves correct before dawn. This was when they planned to attack.

Captain Whitey stayed up talking with Doctor Sunshine and Detective Rabbi. The rest of the men went to sleep. The fire was coals. They talked in low violent tones. The light was red. The sky was black. A top hat of sorts. The stars were random and obscure. The sleeping men snored like frogs. There were crickets. A conspiracy unfolded. Doctor Sunshine and Detective Rabbi both loaded pipes. Captain Whitey watched them. He waited until they both had lit their pipes before he started to speak. His black eyes were red, black mirrors, dead serious. Smoke rose from the pipes. Also from their mouths. They sucked on the stems with their beaks. Holding the pipes in the tips of their wings. Captain Whitey spoke, his words low and angry, he said:

"Dude's a fucking profiteer. We can't let him get away with this shit. I say we destroy his camp completely."

"He did give us the explosives." Doctor Sunshine puffed his pipe. He picked at his chest.

"Yeah, only after stealing all our victuals. I mean, our parlay is stabbed dirt at the moment. Pretty specific if you ask me. I could be wrong, I have been wrong before, but I don't know, you guys tell me." Captain Whitey looked around. Looked Doctor Sunshine and Detective Rabbi in the eye. They both picked at their chests and puffed on their pipes. They both smiled with their beaks at the same time. Detective Rabbi said:

"I say we raid the camp and just see what happens, take them for all they have."

"Yeah, me too. Wreck those bitchholes, tell them who's boss." Doctor Sunshine puffed his pipe. He kept talking. He said:

"Let's sack, dogs, before this water kicks in. Hate to see it go to waste."

"Way ahead of you." Detective Rabbi hopped over next to the fire. He tucked his head under his wing and fell asleep.

"Not the worst idea, see you in a few, Doctor Sunshine, let's parlay, get a couple winks."

"On it, boss. Don't take any wooden nickels." Doctor Sunshine laughed and cuddled next to Detective Rabbi. Captain Whitey sighed and laid down next to his cart. His men liked to panic. The parlay could backfire. He decided to find this amusing. He smiled himself to sleep while staring at the wimpy stars.

60

The stars were still wimpy three hours later. The men started waking up because they had to piss. It was a quiet ritual. Nothing was said. They gathered in a group and made the way to the hill above Daddy Long Legs' camp. They were ready to parlay. The valley was filled with fog. Captain Whitey's men braced themselves for war. Braced for dawn. Captain Whitey had a paper towel tube he was using as a looking glass. Dew gathered on the grass. Captain Whitey and his men were waiting for first light.

61

Dawn came. Not by sight, but by smell. The canal let off a grievous stench, a burning car tire smell mixed with dead carp and something sweet, like mayonnaise. A low fog carried the smell faster than a wind could. A sprung coil of stink. The tides were shifting. The tides that controlled the canal.

Captain Whitey and his men sat on the hill waiting. Captain Whitey passed the paper towel tube around hoping that somebody would see something. The fog obscured the objective. They would have to wait.

Daddy Long Legs' camp was next to a metal recycling center that was next to a highway that was next to a lumberyard that was next to the canal. The hill they were sitting on led down to a sidewalk. This sidewalk was next to an off-ramp that came from the highway. When they first got to the post only two cars had passed in nearly an hour. As the day approached the traffic increased. Soon the traffic became relentless. The fog slowed the traffic. The parlay was stalled. The fog was too thick to see what was happening at Daddy Long Legs' camp and the traffic was too heavy to traverse. Captain Whitey watched this happen in frustration as he took in the canal. He said out loud:

"A fucking moat. Dude's got a moat, I'll be." He was impressed.

"We can flank, sir." Detective Rabbi's optimism was unconvincing.

"Yeah, I don't think so. I say we wait here until the fog clears and watch. There will be no parlay today, sorry, guys." All of Captain Whitey's men flew away. They had no interest in recon. They didn't say goodbye. They just left. Captain Whitey didn't care. He was still interested in how to get into the camp and parlay. He was putting the paper towel tube to his eye when somebody honked their horn. He looked up. A man in his car was holding a five-dollar bill and waving it at Captain Whitey. He yelled, "Here ya go, man!" Captain Whitey was confused. He knew the man was talking to him, so he stood up and walked down and took the money. The man said, "Good luck," and rolled up his window. Captain Whitey stared at the money for a second. He put it in his pocket. The next car drove by, but the car after that rolled his window down and the man handed him a one-dollar bill. Music was blaring from his car and he smelled like cologne. The dollar was cold. The air conditioner was on. Captain Whitey could see that the dollar came from a roll of bills next to a vent. The man rolled his window up without saying anything. Captain Whitey put the dollar in his pocket and started to turn around. To get back to his post. He had every intention of scoping Daddy Long Legs' fortress out. He didn't make it to the grass. There was another honk and a woman was yelling at him. "Sweets!" she yelled. He turned around and she was holding a twenty. He went back. She winked at him and said she dug the uniform. She smelled like perfume. She rolled up her window and drove off.

This went on for an hour. Captain Whitey was bemused at first, but in the end he grew tired of it. He had work to do. If he didn't parlay as per regulations, his men would get upset and mutiny. He had a duty to his crew. He ditched the post. He climbed the hill and got his cart. The fog was gone now. He spied Daddy Long Legs' fortress, but there was nothing to see. It was late in the morning. Now it was hot. He put his paper towel tube in his cart. He put the money from the cars on top of it. There was probably two hundred dollars. The money smelled weird. He didn't like it. He almost threw it in the gutter as he pushed the mail cart to the camp, but he realized it would get some good victuals. Good victuals for a good parlay. His men were probably waiting for him, pissed. They would expect more from a captain.

62

Captain Whitey was back at camp in short order. His men were nowhere to be seen. He parked his mail cart under a tree. The shade was nice. His plan was to gather his men and find a grocery store, acquire some victuals, then parlay. But because his men were gone he felt at a loss. He kind of stood there looking. He would have had some thoughts, but he noticed Runa was down and over, by the bank of the canal, wringing out her underwear. She was squatting. Her hair like squirrels running around her shoulders. Her naked ass splayed out. She seemed to be rubbing her asshole on the tip of a branch of a bush behind her. She seemed to be birdless herself. Captain Whitey shot off a few hearts, like a cartoon, they floated into the air and popped. His own heartbeat through his chest. An action of love.

Captain Whitey walked over. He adjusted his boner so it went straight up. He made sure the tip was hidden. This meant he had to untuck his shirt. She noticed he was coming over. She also noticed his attempt to hide his boner. She said as much:

"What-cha got there, sailor? Hiding the plank?" She kept scratching her asshole on the branch. She put her damp underwear in her pocket and smiled at Captain Whitey. "Do me a favor, scratch my asshole for me, I don't know if I have worms or what, but this branch ain't doing the trick."

Captain Whitey scratched her asshole. His fingernails were long. She moaned. She told him, "That's the ticket, the itch is deeper." Captain Whitey put his finger in her asshole. He couldn't feel any worms. She smelled like wet paint and dirty ass. Captain Whitey couldn't take it anymore. He pulled down his pants and fucked her in the open. Her hands in the dirt, her ass in the air. Luckily there was nobody around to see it. He came fast and fell over. Runa stayed as she was, her ass in the air, itching. Captain Whitey still scratching her asshole. He said:

"Runa."

"Does it feel like worms? I feel like I got worms. Can you check?"

"I can check, it doesn't feel like worms though, let me check." Captain Whitey sat up. He spread Runa's butt cheeks. Her ass was dirty and red. He did his best to open her butthole and look inside. He didn't see any worms. He slapped her butt cheek and said, "Think you're just dirty, clean your ass."

"You sure?"

"I'm certain. What you wiping with, just leaves?"

"Yeah, leaves, I guess, what else? I'm not a millionaire. What do you use, socks?"

"I just shit in the canal."

"Then what?"

"I don't know, water."

"Fucking boys. Fuckers, you got it easy."

"I got money, lots of it, I can get you toilet paper."

"Serious?" Runa pushed Captain Whitey's hand from her ass and stood up. She took the damp underwear from her pocket and put them on. Captain Whitey smelled his finger. It stank. He went to the edge of the canal and rinsed it off. He smelled it again. Half the smell was still there. In a fit of love he kissed Runa on the cheek. She smiled and kicked him on the ankle. They walked over to Captain Whitey's mail cart. It was noon and the shade was gone.

63

Captain Whitey knew that money was important. But it was not important to him. The idea was that he could take the money and get things and then the things he got would get other things and then those things would get him more things, and then more things, and more things. But then Runa, and her itchy asshole.

Runa blew. Captain Whitey watched her leave. He smelled his finger again and made a mental note to buy her toilet paper. He rinsed his finger again, but the smell remained exactly as it was. He wiped it on some grass. He forgot about it. The sun became overwhelming. He frowned and looked for some shade. No shade. He shrugged. He tucked his shirt back in. He went to his camp to wait for his men. Ten minutes went by. Nobody. Nothing. He got so hot that the sweat from his face started stinging his eyes. He sat down next to his mail cart hoping that sitting down would make him cooler. It didn't. He was standing up to go look for some shade when Doctor Sunshine flew in. He had a smile on his beak and his nose holes were covered in white powder. Captain Whitey sat back down.

Doctor Sunshine looked intense. He talked fast. He smelled like gasoline and laxative. He kept biting at his tail feathers and looking from side to side. He was pacing and hopping at the same time. He was making Captain Whitey nervous. Captain Whitey said as much:

"Cool it, Sunshine, what's up? You're making me nervous."

"What? What's up with you? You calm down, you're making me nervous." Doctor Sunshine started rubbing his beak with his wing. Looking at the ground and then staring at Captain Whitey.

"What the hell, man? Where you been? Where are the guys? I got new thoughts." Captain Whitey stared back. Doctor Sunshine got nervous and flew into the air. He landed again and hopped. He paced and rubbed his beak.

"No, man, I tell you what, that dude's cool, we should let him be." Doctor Sunshine used his toe/claw to draw something in the dirt. He scratched it out. He looked up at Captain Whitey and smiled with his beak.

"What dude? I don't know any dudes, you dudes are the only dudes I know."

"Long Legs."

"Daddy Long Legs? Seriously?" Captain Whitey pulled a blade of grass from the ground. The root came with it. He put the root end in his mouth without thinking. It tasted like dirt. He shook his head.

"Yeah, man, the dude is loaded. His party is awesome, you should come!"

"Yeah, but you remember that we were about to invade his camp this morning! He's not a friend, remember? You guys are insane!"

"All I know is, he's got hot babes, good blow, and a sweet pad. Be cool for once in your life."

"Fucking hell." Doctor Sunshine flew away. Captain Whitey sat there stunned. There were a few necks he would like to ring. Doctor Sunshine's of course, but he seemed high. He was used to high people, so he couldn't hold it against him. But the rest of those jerks. Did they really just join a party at the enemy's house?

The sun beat down on Captain Whitey's head like a wrestler giving him a full nelson. Illegal and releaseless. He wiped his eyes. He would go to this party and tell them what's up. He stood up and pushed his mail cart back towards Daddy Long Legs' post, under and near the highway. He was hot and angry. He smelled his finger hoping that he would calm down, but Runa's ass smell just gave him philosophical ideas.

65

The whole walk to the party Captain Whitey talked to himself. He was going to give it them, his men, tell them how it was, is. "Fucking shit," he said, "and another thing, you better get right, I tell you.

"I mean, I tell you, ya know? Don't be so like, I don't know, whatever. Damn! Shit's pretty cool, but then, but then, I mean, shit, know what I mean? Those guys, them guys, fucking jerks, I tell you. You ever think about that? Yeah, fucking last time, I tell you who. Well, when, next time? No, I don't think so."

Captain Whitey stopped at one point to pick up a rock. The rock was pretty. He threw it at a sign. The rock missed the sign. He stamped the ground and yelled. He felt weird after this. He felt foolish and smiled. Maybe he himself was high from the sun. The sun was hot. Relentless.

66

The party was in an alley. Behind a dumpster. Captain Whitey thought it was quite goofy to attend this party. Frustrating in fact. Most of the men at this party were his enemies. Had he not just sat on a hill across the street casing the joint? What? Just this morning?

He was in a bad mood when he got there. It took him ten minutes to cross the street which earlier in the day he had called a moat. He had to race between cars to cross. He got honked at and yelled at. By the skin of my teeth, he thought when he got across. He was holding his mail cart like a baby antelope. Protecting it. He had to jump onto the sidewalk to avoid being run over. He was sweaty. And hot. And in no mood. He put his mail cart down. He scanned the parking lot for danger. There was none. He looked to where he was going. He resigned himself. Whatever he would find behind that dumpster he would do his best to agree with.

This thought was pointless. Nothing could prepare himself for what came next. The twenty seconds that it took Captain Whitey to push his mail cart to the back of the dumpster were possibly the most peaceful and focused moments of his short and brutal life. It was a blanket execution, both because he didn't know what was coming and because he was aligned with the outcome. Only an astronaut would understand. Or a cosmonaut. Or a bull rider.

There were short bursts of noise coming from behind the dumpster. Laughter and music. He parked his mail cart and took a breath. He shook his head. The heat like a razor blade slicing his scalp. He braced himself and walked around to the back. His hands were balled into fists. He was ready to strike, just in case the party was a trap. The party was not a trap. The party was a party. A crazy party that took Captain Whitey a moment to process. He stood there with his hands making fists. His mouth open. His eyeballs cocked and molested. Vacillating between burnt match heads and sliced black olives.

Detective Rabbi was doing a keg stand. Two crows were holding his feet. They were yelling, "Chug, chug, chug!" Doctor Sunshine was laughing and holding a beer in the air. He was standing next to a pile of cocaine. On a smashed beer can. On top of a log. He was screaming, "Tell them Large Marge sent you!" Moiler was passed out under a piece of burlap. Bunker was making out with some weird bird with a long neck. Finch was smoking a cigarette and trying to look cool. He had sunglasses on. There was some band doing jazz. Two crows, a pigeon and a seagull. The seagull was a drummer. The pigeon was playing bass. One of the crows had a guitar. The other one sang:

"You think you're fancy, I think you stink, I want to romance ye, and put it in your pink. Cause we are heading, in a new, direction." There was a dance move. A feather adjustment. A bob, and then a tail wag. The song moved on, but Captain Whitey didn't notice. He was looking at Runa. She was sitting next to Daddy Long Legs. He didn't know what jealousy was, but he felt it. Daddy Long Legs was smiling. Bobbing his long neck. His arm/wing around Runa. They had drinks in front of them. On a log. Captain Whitey went over. His hand was a fist. His right hand. He was about to punch Daddy Long Legs in the mouth. Daddy Long Legs held his wings/hands up and said:

"Come on, man, what the fuck?" He pecked at Runa's neck and looked back at Captain Whitey. Smiling.

"The fuck is you are next to Runa, what the fuck, Runa?" Captain Whitey was in love with Runa. He was perplexed. Runa said:

"Yeah, sorry, Whitey, Long Legs' got property, what do you got? Camp and a parlay? Ha! Leave something to the imagination."

"Yeah, but his shit is a dumpster," Captain Whitey said.

"A dumpster is something," Runa said.

"A sweetass dumpster," Daddy Long Legs said.

"Stand up, Daddy Long Legs, I want to punch your stupid face. I might be wrong, but I think you're an asshole."

"We'll see about that." Daddy Long Legs stood up. Captain Whitey punched Daddy Long Legs in his long stork neck two times. He fell to the ground. Runa stood up and screamed. The party stopped for a second and looked over. Captain Whitey stood there angry. His fists clenched. Runa ran away. Captain Whitey was jealous and angry and resentful. There was regret as well. He didn't know if he should chase after Runa or wait for Daddy Long Legs to wake up so he could punch him in the neck again. He decided to wait.

67

The party was over. Captain Whitey's men flew over as soon as they understood what was happening. Everyone else scattered. Daddy Long Legs was lying on his side. There was blood coming out of his beak. He was breathing. Captain Whitey was clenching his fists still. Looking down. His men were standing around the body, hopping. They were drunk and high and excited. Sun stroked their bodies, a full-body fire-massage. They were hot and just as angry as their captain. Doctor Sunshine spit on the ground. He said:

"I say we string the fucker up."

"Don't think we got enough rope, neck like that," Moiler said, while wobbling. He wiped some drool from his beak.

"I say we tuck him into bed, guys, he don't look so good." Finch said. He looked scared. The men all laughed. Finch wasn't joking. He flew away.

"Pussy!" Detective Rabbi yelled. "I agree, let's string the fucker up, gettin' on your girl like that, Cappy."

"Only solution," Moiler said.

"Only solution," Bunker repeated.

Captain Whitey came out of his anger-induced trance. For a brief moment he was just looking down at a knocked-out stork lying on the ground with blood coming out of its mouth surrounded by four bobbing pigeons behind a dumpster in Brooklyn. He was confused. What the hell, he thought. But then a breeze came by and stirred up Runa's smell that was clinging to Daddy Long Legs. The smell wafted to his nose. He was enraged again. He said:

"What the fuck you talking about? I should hang all you motherfuckers up for coming to this party in the first place! I'm in my rights, man! This is close to mutiny! This fucker's the enemy! Regards me, regards me now! I am cutting rations for all you hemp-sliverin', salt-tight, tooth-broken, lubber-lovin' cunts! As God be me witness! You will always be hungerin'. As for this pencil-necked alabaster cunt, I prithee thee, he be walkin' the plank, tie him up boys!"

The men were dejected. They set to work tying Daddy Long Legs up. They weren't drunk anymore. Or high. They used strands of a mop that were wrapped around the wheels of the dumpster to tie him up. When they were finished Captain Whitey told them to pick him up. They put the stork on their shoulders. His head stayed on the ground. They carried him feet first behind Captain Whitey. Captain Whitey walking away. Two men on each side. The head dragging behind.

They crossed the street easy. Traffic was at a standstill. On the other side they took a shortcut and walked over the hill, dragging the stork's head along the grass. The river was across a parking lot. The parking lot was empty. They got to the dock with very little effort. The men were sweating though. It was hot. They were unhappy. Captain Whitey was still angry with them. The dock was abandoned. It was old and warped. Grey. They navigated holes. They stopped. Captain Whitey ordered them to put the stork down and untie him. The men did. They stood there waiting. Waiting for Daddy Long Legs to wake up. He never did. Captain Whitey ordered Doctor Sunshine to get some water. He left and came back with a pail. Captain Whitey nodded. Doctor Sunshine threw the water in Daddy Long Legs' face. He woke up and sputtered. He threw his long neck into the air and said:

"Where the…?"

"Your ass is grass, Long Legs." Captain Whitey smiled.

"But I…." Daddy Long Legs was sitting up now.

"But you what? Like a little plank in your tank? I got one right here. March him out boys!"

The men marched Daddy Long Legs to the edge of the dock. They stood there holding him. Captain Whitey said:

"Any last words, Long Legs? I'm sure to write them in my diarrhea." The men all laughed.

"Fuck you. Fuck all you bitches. And most of all, fuck your parlay!"

"Say 'hi' to Davy Jones, you swarthy dog. Sink him boys!" The men threw Daddy Long Legs into the river. He sank for a while, but then he realized he was a water bird and swam to the surface. He flew away yelling," Fuck you! And fuck Davy Jones!"

His men were horrified. Captain Whitey just smiled. He had a plan. The plan was an egg. The egg just hatched.

68

The men were dejected as they made their way back to camp. They were waiting for a lashing. They were now on rations, which was meaningless considering they could just fly off and get food wherever they found it, but they felt bad about letting Captain Whitey down. Had any of them had the guts to just look him in the eye they would have seen how little he cared. The glint he possessed was so easy, so open and giving that he looked like a different man, a stronger man. A man on the verge. A man on the verge of something great.

But, alas, they sulked.

The late afternoon turned into evening as Captain Whitey's men puttered around mending camp and looking forlorn. Captain Whitey took no notice. He had his own mending to do. He also had no sympathy for his men's anguish. They brought it on themselves. He would probably forgive them in a day or two, but for now he needed their full commitment, and if that meant that they thought he was extremely angry with them, well, so be it. Loyalty was important to Captain Whitey, but at the moment he needed respect. There is no greater catalyst to respect than fear, and fear is biological.

Captain Whitey spent the evening counting money, one hundred and forty-six dollars. Making lists of things he would need:

Beans, twelve cans, twelve dollars.

Salt pork, twelve pounds, twelve dollars.

Hardtack, twelve boxes, twelve dollars.

Cheese, six pounds, twelve dollars.

Vitamin C powder, twelve packets, twelve dollars.

Vegetable bouillon, twelve boxes, twelve dollars.

Salt, twelve pounds, twelve dollars.

Chipped beef, twelve cans, twelve dollars.

Condensed milk, both sweetened and unsweetened, six of each, twelve dollars.

Sugar, six pounds, twelve dollars.

Spices, pepper, anise, cumin, dried garlic, six ounces, twelve dollars.

Onions, twelve pounds, twelve dollars.

He had two dollars left. Good. He picked up a branch and a leaf and wrote in his log:

Day Eight. Things are going good. Parlay is within eyesight. Had to teach the men a lesson about respect and loyalty. Sunshine is taking it the hardest. Overheard him talking of leaving. I doubt his sincerity. Maybe tomorrow I drop the charade. Daddy Long Legs has been taken care of. Runa is gone. My heart feels broken, but the parlay will benefit. Tomorrow is a big day. I must rest. The sky is red tonight. Good omen.

Captain Whitey put his log into the mail cart. Also the money and the list of victuals. He stood up and walked down to his men. They were looking glum. Sitting around a wimpy fire, hardly smoking and barely talking. He issued an edict:

"Tomorrow at dawn."

"Yes, captain!" They all stood up and saluted him.

"Good, good. Get some rest."

Captain Whitey went back to his mail cart and made his bed. He got in it. He stared at the sky. His hands under his head. Night was approaching quickly. He watched airplanes and thought about Runa. He loved her, but she did him wrong. And with Daddy Long Legs nonetheless. That guy's a goon, he thought. He didn't know what to do. Should he kick her ass to the curb? Find her and take her back? He was undecided as he fell asleep. He dreamed about horrible things that had actually happened in his life. When he woke up he was more committed than ever to the parlay. There was something about the dreams that made the parlay more real, more tactile and calloused. He couldn't remember the dreams. Not exactly, at least. There was a bathroom and a window and a feeling of hope.

69

The dawn crackled with kindling. The men were up and starting a fire. Making coffee and getting ready. They didn't know what to plan for, so they planned for everything. Knives were sharpened. Satchels were packed. Finch whittled a poking stick. When there was nothing left to prepare they sat around the fire, waiting.

Fog covered the camp. The smell of the canal hung low and rancid. The fire became coals as the sun took the fog into the sky to make clouds, and with it, the stink. Dark and white to bright and white.

When the men could finally see they looked around for Captain Whitey. He was nowhere. His mail cart was gone. Maybe he left them, they all thought, but nobody said anything. An hour went by before he showed up. He was whistling. The men all looked stupid. They could only take so much torture. And since they were birds, well, even less. Captain Whitey laughed at the looks on their faces. He decided to drop the charade and forgive them. He said:

"Look at you sad sacks! Cheer up! I was never really mad at you. You're all a bunch of assholes, I knew this going in, c'mon, we got a parlay to conclude!"

His men were suspect. Normally they would have just hopped on his mail cart and parlayed, but he had taken it too far. Captain Whitey approached them. They recoiled like beaten dogs. He stopped. He realized a speech was in order. They respected him now, but they didn't trust him anymore. He gathered his thoughts and became glorious. He said:

"Doctor Sunshine, you salty dog, have we not been in this parlay from the beginning? Were you not there for the attack on the dumpster parlay?"

"Ay, Cappy."

"And you, Detective Rabbi, did I not sew your wounds shut after that same parlay?"

"Ay, Cappy."

"And Moiler, sweet Moiler, did you not save me from the prison?"

"Ay, Cappy."

"And Beeper, did you not throw up in the bushes when we threw the party for the babes?"

"Ay, Cappy."

"And Bunker, was your name not The Talker when I met you? Does that not mean anything to you?"

"I mean, ay, Cappy, if you know what I mean."

"I know what you mean, Bunker. And Finch, I know how hard you try. Your bravery is truly heroic. Are you aware of this, mate?"

"Ay, Cappy." Captain Whitey took a moment. He looked down at the coals that were once a fire. He looked back up. He spoke slowly and with conviction. He said:

"Good. Good. Great, even. Great!

"Men, and you are all men of great stature, so I do not say this lightly. Men, we are about to embark on the greatest parlay since Blackbeard took the Bahamas. A parlay of a lifetime. A parlay that will last a lifetime. A hundred lifetimes. A hundred wives bearing a hundred children. A gold nugget for every feather on your body. Rivers of molten gold flowing from the mountains of jewels that reach to the diamond stars that will light up the universe. You will never sleep again, my friends! The sky will be too bright, the women too beautiful and loving, the food too sumptuous, the cries of pleasure, too loud.

"I tell you this now, so you can prepare yourselves. So you can see the world as I see it, beautiful and fortive. Do you understand?"

"Yes, Cappy!" They all stood up and said this in unison.

"Parlay!" Captain Whitey screamed as loud as he could.

"Parlay!" his men echoed.

"Parlay!"

"Parlay!" and then in unison:

"Parlay! Parlay! Parlay! Parlay!"

There was a frenzy and then confusion. They all got so excited they flew away. Captain Whitey sighed. He shrugged his shoulders. He pushed his mail cart towards the grocery store.

70

The morning was early. The parking lot of the grocery store was empty. It was surrounded by hedges. Captain Whitey hid his mail cart in the hedges. He made sure he hide his list and his money. He waited for a second, just in case his men would show up. They didn't. He walked to the entrance. There was a metal fence made out of square tubing. He could get in, but the shopping carts couldn't get out. It was painted grey. He pulled a cart from the linear stack. The front wheels didn't work right so he pushed it aside and took out another. This one too was no good. He took out another, and another. None of them seemed to be working right, but now there was no space to keep testing. His solution was to lift the defective carts and put them on the other side of the fence. He did this with alacrity and grace. It took him ten tries before somebody came out and yelled at him. "Hey, stop that!" they yelled. Luckily he had found one that worked. He smiled and pushed the grocery cart inside.

71

The grocery store was massive. There were twelve aisles. He stood there for a second taking it in. The employees looked at him with a profound eye towards derision. He was very dirty. He smelled too. Like dirt and birds. He was also wearing a mailman's uniform. He didn't notice the staring. He looked at his list. Beans. The aisles had lists themselves. Aisle six said beans. He pushed the grocery cart towards aisle six.

Beans! There were so many beans! Dried beans. Canned beans. Black beans. Fava beans. White beans. Refried beans. Pinto beans. Garbanzo beans. Kidney beans. Navy beans. He thought the beans would be easy. He stood there for ten minutes trying to decide. In the end, he went with navy beans because they had a nautical theme. But they were a dollar and nineteen cents. He went with black beans after all. Ninety-nine cents a can. He put twelve cans in his grocery cart. Now he had an extra twelve cents.

The next item was salt pork. The meat section was in the back of the store. Looking at the meats made him hungry, so he grabbed twelve pounds as fast as he could. They came in two-pound hunks. A dollar and ninety eight cents a piece. Twelve more cents. Almost a quarter.

None of the aisles had hardtack. The closest thing was crackers. Generic saltines. He didn't save any money, in fact, he was now over budget by fifteen cents and his cart was almost full. He became overwhelmed. This was too much stuff. He wished his men were here so they could help him think. He decided to find the cheese and regroup. The cheese, however, was worse than the beans. There was Swiss cheese, American cheese, Gouda, cheddar cheese, white cheddar cheese, smoked Gouda, Parmesan, shredded cheese, brie, blue cheese, Pepper Jack cheese, huge blocks of cheese, small chunks of cheese, wedges, squares, circles, mozzarella cheese, Italian cheese, French cheese, cheese from Dublin, cheese in plastic wrapping. Captain Whitey couldn't take it. He grabbed a huge block of cheddar cheese and put it in the cart and sat down on the edge of the refrigerator. He would have fallen asleep except his butt got cold. He decided to pay for the groceries and put them in his mail cart. He would take a break after that and hopefully the men would show up and they would help him finish the shopping.

72

Captain Whitey pushed the grocery cart to a checkout aisle. There were six checkout aisles. Only two were open. One was available. The other one had an elderly woman arguing with the cashier about weekly bargains. Captain Whitey chose the one that was not occupied. He put his groceries on the conveyor belt. This was fun for him. The victuals seemed like they were on some sort of adventure. He got really excited when the cashier started putting the groceries in plastic bags. These were fresh plastic bags. Mint condition! He paid. The cashier's lips were tucked into his teeth for the whole interaction. Captain Whitey didn't notice. He was excited about the bags. He put the groceries back into the grocery cart and pushed it out to the metal fence enclosure. He stopped. He was suddenly trapped. His mail cart was in the hedges. His groceries were in the grocery cart on this side of the fence. He didn't know what to do. He couldn't just leave the groceries behind and go get the cart, could he? Somebody would steal them. Daddy Long Legs perhaps, or one of his men. But he couldn't take the grocery cart to his mail cart, or could he? He tested the weight of the cart. Not too bad. He thought that if he got a hold down low enough… a second later he was pushing the grocery cart towards his mail cart. Whistling.

73

His men were waiting for him when he got to the hedges. They seemed excited to see him. He opened a box of crackers and took out a sleeve. He opened the sleeve and dumped the cracker squares on the ground. His men pecked. And cooed. They were hungry and happy.

Captain Whitey took his mail cart from the hedges and started to pack it. He decided this was foolish. He unpacked it and put it on top of the grocery cart. He made sure it was secure. He watched his men eat for a while. When they seemed fed he said, "Ok, let's roll, there's plenty more where that came from." He pushed the grocery cart through the hedges and down the sidewalk. His men rode on the edge of the grocery cart. They thought it was fun. The wheels were harder than the mail cart, so the ride was bumpy. They laughed and hooted the whole way back. Beeper got sick and threw up. He had to lay down. Nobody made fun of him though. This made Captain Whitey smile. He was a big fan of people being nice to each other. Ten blocks and ten minutes later, they were back at the camp.

Captain Whitey ordered Moiler to build a fire. A large fire. They would feast tonight. He ordered Detective Rabbi and Doctor Sunshine to prepare a salt pork and a can of beans for cooking. They set straight to work. He ordered Bunker to dig a hole, one foot by one foot by one foot, five feet from the fire. He handed him a spoon. He ordered Beeper to help. Aye, aye! He then took Finch aside and out of earshot. He said:

"Finch."

"Aye, sir!"

"Find Runa and Maybellene and Princess Toots. Bring them back here."

"Sir?"

"You're a sensitive guy, Finch, you should understand this."

"Aye, sir."

"Haul ass."

"Aye!" Finch flew away as fast as he could. He had purpose in his heart.

It was a long day so far, and hardly even noon. Captain Whitey found some shade and sat down. Day nine, he thought, but now we got victuals. He decided to look at the clouds. He fell asleep while trying to get comfortable.

74

The nap was hard and deep, a bucket being dropped into a well. A sinking feeling. A tipping over and submergence. A new gravity. Cool, wet and heavy. Blackness. Without dreams. Closing his eyes was the easy part, gravity helped, opening them back up, well, the bucket was full. Gravity disagreed. The bucket was full. The rope resisted. His eyelids straining. Stretching against the weight. The rope. His eyelids. And now the heat. A new wetness. Sweat. Sleeping sweat. The inertia of reality. A tipping over of re-emergence. Lightness. Flooding waters into the gutter of human knowledge. Flooding light. Awake.

75

Captain Whitey was awake. His nap was short. He felt better. He was hot and sweaty though. The shade had moved as he slept. The sun was beating on him. He sat up and looked around. The shade had not gone far. He scooted over into it. He watched his men tending the fire and digging the hole. Preparing the salt pork and opening the beans. They seemed happy enough, although he wasn't too concerned with their happiness. He watched them work. When the fire was nothing but coals he stood up. He didn't know if the birds were reading his mind or if they naturally understood that they should let the fire burn to coals. Maybe he ordered them to? He couldn't remember.

He found a large flat stone. He brought it with him to the fire. Nobody said anything to him. He didn't say anything either. He put the stone on the ground. His men used the spoon Bunker had been using to dig the hole to put coals on the stone. Captain Whitey put the coals in the hole that Bunker dug. He took the stone back to the fire. His men loaded more coals. Captain Whitey took the stone back to the hole that Bunker dug. He did this two more times.

The hole was hot and ready for the ham. Detective Rabbi and Doctor Sunshine were ready with the salt pork. They lifted it up and dropped it on the coals. It sizzled. Bunker covered the ham with the dirt that was in a mound next to the hole. The can of beans was ready too, but the birds couldn't open it. They brought it over to Captain Whitey. He cracked the can and peeled the lid back. The snapping noise made his men fly away. They flew back moments later. It took all four of them to lift the can and put it on top of the remaining coals. Some feathers got singed.

There was nothing to do now except wait. Captain Whitey dumped a sleeve of crackers on the ground and decided to go for a walk. His men cooed and pecked at the crackers. He felt a strange flatness as he watched them. Zero emotion. He couldn't tell if he didn't care or maybe he was just being philosophical. Maybe both. It didn't matter. He was blocks away before he even thought about thinking about it. By then he had other things on his mind.

76

The parlay felt ruined. He had promised his men a feast, but that was a lie. They didn't eat pork, and they didn't eat beans. The feast was for Runa. He wondered if his men knew that. They probably did. They were just being subordinate. Loyal. This thought made him ill. How could love get in the way of a parlay? His men had proven to be fickle, however. How could he trust them? But he loved them just as much as he loved Runa. Didn't he? Did they love him? They must, right? Did they trust him? Could they? He himself was fickle. He was thinking these thoughts when he found himself next to a deli in Ditmas Park. There were three pigeons he had never met before hopping around. The sidewalk was littered with bread crumbs. There should have been more birds around, but this was the bad part of town, for pigeons. Cats. Lots of cats. These birds had balls. They also knew who Captain Whitey was. Punching Daddy Long Legs in the neck and then making him walk the plank had made him famous. They greeted him with excitement. They asked him to join them. He did. He sat down, leaning against the side of the building. He was handed a beer. The pigeons stopped bobbing around and pecking. They leaned against the wall themselves. The birds were cool. Captain Whitey felt cool. He cracked the beer open. He held it up. "Cheers," he said. They said, "Salut!" They had their own beers suddenly. Where they came from Captain Whitey didn't know. He was starting to feel insane. He ignored this feeling. He said:

"Nice spread, it's like this every day?"

"Mostly. The owner of this deli likes us. Tough feed though. The cats are vicious around these parts," Bobby said. Bobby was called Bobby because he bobbed so much. He was bobbing as he talked. His head. There was a meter to his talking. Like a metronome.

"We lost two friends just yesterday," Colonel Popcorn said. He was small and white. Very white. And puffy. Like a popcorn kernel.

"God. Poor souls. Amigos!" Jelly Beans Junior said. He put his beer in the air. He had spots. He looked like candy to Captain Whitey. The spots were black and brown. The rest of his feathers were kind of blue.

"Amigos!" they all yelled, Captain Whitey included. Then they drank.

They drank for a while. A long time. Sitting down leaning against the wall. Next to the deli. The bread spread out before them. The sun rustic. The mood somber. Talking.

"Those cats are a problem, ya know, they come out of nowhere. It's like they have little whispers on their feet, one second your pecking on a juicy bread-chunked nugget and the next second you're gone, like a feather in the wind, a bloody blood-soaked feather, flapping in the fucking breeze, ya dig?" Bobby had tears in his eyes. He drank some beer and choked back his emotions. Looking into the distance.

"Oh Papi, don't I know it," Jelly Beans Junior was full of emotions himself. "I forgot to tell you guys! There is a family of those pendejos over in that lot over there. I seen 'em from the fence just yesterday." He pointed with his wing to the corner across the street. "They had a mouse cornered, I couldn't watch, his ass was grass. We gotta do something, I mean, we can't live this way. Fuck them pendejos."

"Salut!" They raised their beers.

"Why not just move to a different corner?" Captain Whitey was trying to help. His words were inciting though. Colonel Popcorn got upset. He said:

"Move! Move? Did the Aztec move when Cortez and his horrible army invaded Mexico? No. They strung his men up by their ankles and ripped their skin off! And Pancho Villa, did he move when the Americans invaded his beloved Chihuahua? Hell no! He got an agent and made some fucking movies, that's what he did! And now he's got a tasty tequila named after him. We were born here, we will fucking die here! Viva!"

"Viva!" the birds yelled.

Captain Whitey suddenly felt like an outsider. These birds were in their own world. He didn't want revolution, he wanted to parlay. He didn't know how to say this. He stood up and walked away. He got to the corner and looked in the trash can. The only thing of interest was a receipt from Mr. Smile for two dollars and ninety-nine cents. He put it in his pocket and walked on.

The sun was on the horizon now. The day was over. Captain Whitey's thoughts moved back to his men. The ham must be cooked by now. Hopefully Finch found Runa and Princess Toots and Maybellene, and had brought them back to the camp. He wouldn't know this until he got back to the camp. It was a long walk. He decided to haul ass.

79

The thoughts in Captain Whitey's head were not pleasant as he walked his way back towards the camp. He made a point of turning the lid of every fire hydrant he passed. This gave him comfort. That is, as long as the metal crosses would spin. Sometimes they didn't. He didn't understand why this happened. He knew there was a special tool that firemen used to make the hydrants work, but why did most of them spin with a pleasant metal grinding motion and some of them seemed to be stuck, even glued, to the top of the hydrants? And why were they crosses? And what possibly could the tool look like that removed the crosses and gave the firemen access to the valve that turned the water on? And why were some of them stuck? And was this a good thing, or a bad thing?

There wasn't a single answer. No logic. He hoped that a fire truck would come by and he could flag it down and ask, but he was taking side streets. No fire truck came by. At one point he walked by a station house and stopped some guy that was walking by and asked him. The guy just squinted his eyes and walked away. Whitey tried to think about this, but then his mind went back to the cooking ham and the idea of Runa. He said to himself:

"If only I could hug the universe, I would be decent, at least for an hour. hen victuals would rain down like manna from heaven, like snowflakes of dried honey I could catch on my tongue, yeah, that would be alright, I could find my way then. Runa would love me, I would finally be decent. Decent."

Captain Whitey found himself punching a brick wall. He felt scared for a second. Lost. He tried to smell a smell. There were no smells. Sounds. Only sounds. His hands punching the wall. What the hell, he thought. Then nothing. Then the smell of blood and brick.

When Captain Whitey got back to camp his hands hurt. Runa was sitting with her legs crossed next to a fire. Princess Toots and Maybellene where on her shoulders. She looked bored and angry. His men were digging the ham up and paid no attention to his arrival. Finch flew over and screamed in his ear:

"I did good, Cappy! I did real good! See! See!" Captain Whitey recoiled and shooed him away. His ear now hurt. Finch became dejected and flew towards the canal. The men looked up but paid him no mind. Finch landed on a branch in a nearby tree and pouted. He stared at Captain Whitey. 'I try so hard and this is how he repays me' were the thoughts going through Finch's mind. Captain Whitey watched this happen, he tried to care, but he didn't. He had his own thoughts to think about. He sat down next to Runa and said:

"Nice fire, hot log, right?" Captain Whitey smiled.

"Shut it, a-hole, why the hell you drag me to this lousy boner-fest, you're like a wimpy worm without any teeth." She spit on the fire. She adjusted her hair until it looked like a weird curly hat.

"I don't know, we got a ham." Captain Whitey felt so insecure he started picking grass and putting it on his knee.

"Good for you, you suck, why did you punch my boyfriend in the neck?"

"Long Legs is your boyfriend, since when?" Captain Whitey stopped playing with the grass.

"Since whenever, why do you care? He knows things you don't." Princess Toots flew from one shoulder to the other. Maybellene scooted over and bit at her chest feathers.

"That's bullshit, I know things. I know everything, ever think of that?"

"A woman's body is a sensitive machine, you need to lube the oils, hmm-hmm, take a note or two, you brute. Be cool for once in your life." Runa stood up. Her birds flew away and landed next to Captain Whitey's men.

"Don't do this." Captain Whitey's eyes looked like shiny black olives.

"Do what?" Runa knew what the question meant. She didn't care. Captain Whitey had a lousy parlay. Daddy Long Legs was long and strong. He could satisfy. Runa made a face that could harvest raspberries, tender but on purpose. Gentle. She yelled:

"Come on, girls!" Her birds joined her as she walked away. Captain Whitey stared at his hands. He smelled them. They smelled like blood and bricks. He looked at his men. They were struggling with the ham. He watched Runa walk away. He felt a sadness. He stood up and walked over to his men. They were happy to see him. There was a smell of hot ham and dirty feathers. His sadness disappeared. He touched the ham.

The ham was hot.

81

"You're doing it wrong!" Doctor Sunshine was yelling at Captain Whitey. "You're gonna… "

"Gonna what?" Captain Whitey was taking the ham out of the hole they dug.

"It's too hot! You're gonna drop it!"

"It's not too hot, I got hands like steel!" He lifted the ham up and dropped it because it was too hot.

"See! Now it's dirty, you maniac! Get a stick, let's get a stick."

"Fuck sticks, I can use my foot." He kicked the ham. The ham fell apart. "Whoops."

"Whoops? You're the worst! The ham is ruined!"

"It ain't ruined, we can rinse it off, hand me some water."

"What water? You drunk?"

"I'm not drunk, you are." Captain Whitey was indeed drunk. But it wasn't a regular drunk, he was stupid. Foolish with heartache. He kicked the ham again. The ham fell apart some more. He sneered and walked away. He walked over to his mail cart and picked it up. He dumped all of the contents out. "Victuals, my ass!" He righted the mail cart and pushed it into the black streets. He needed to be alone. He left a pile of groceries and paper money. The birds didn't care because he had stopped thinking about them. He pushed the mail cart a block away. He sat down next to the canal and tried to think. Thinking was hard at the moment. He had too many emotions. He got tired. He fell asleep.

82

Morning came without meaning. Captain Whitey had no dreams. He was hot and sweaty. His legs were angry. His body was angry. He felt annoyed. His head was angry. There was grass under his head. Grass under his legs. Bugs crawling. His mouth was dry. He opened his eyes for a moment. The sun was too much. He closed his eyes and went back to sleep.

Sleep changed nothing. It made it worse. The day was hotter. His broken heart hurt. He was thirsty and he couldn't complete thoughts. The words "why not" entered his head, followed by the words "what not," then followed by the words "wine knot," then "want tot." What's a wine knot tater tot? It's a potato, top knot. What's a top knot, butter pot?

Focus was beyond his capacity. Words were letters only. He couldn't stop thinking about them. Letters. They were everywhere. He was restless. Pushing his mail cart. Relentless. He saw the word "curb" on a sign about dogs. Cunts Under Rusty Bridges. Which led to See You Next Tuesday. Which led to C U Next Tuesday. Which led to CUNY. City University of New York. City University. City Uni. Cy Tuny. Sight Any. See Something Say Something. He said these words out loud as he dug through trash cans. Looking for anything that made sense.

Half a hot-dog in a tinfoil wrapper made sense. A black sock covered in mustard did not. A dishwasher's paper hat made sense. A bag full of cigarette butts and tissue did not. And the words. Butts. Boners Under Tender Toys. Toys In Babeland. Babe Baby Bottle Rocket. BBB. BBC. British Broadcasting Cunt. C U Next Tuesday!

Captain Whitey was exhausted with words. He couldn't help himself though. They made him feel better. There was a moment when he forced himself to stop. He became so anxious that he ran as fast as he could down the block before the feeling went away. This made him sweaty. He remembered he was thirsty. Two blocks later he found a half-filled bottle of water at the bottom of a trash can. He drank it and sat down. The lid was covered in muck and the lip tasted like lipstick, but he put the empty bottle in the mail cart anyway. It was at this moment that he noticed that his crew was riding on the top of his mail cart. He said:

"Whoa! When did you guys get here?"

"We've been here the whole time, sir." Detective Rabbi was smoking a pipe. The men were at ease.

"I just got here," Finch said. He looked winded.

"Fucking Finch, you salty dog!" The men all laughed. Captain Whitey shook his head. He felt normal again, but had some questions. He smiled. He played with a stray string on his pants.

84

Captain Whitey felt better again. His heart was no longer broken. Words were no longer a problem. He let his entire crew ride on his shoulders. He whistled their favorite song. The "Battle Hymn of the Republic." He pushed his mail cart down the sidewalk. Glory, glory, hallelujah. Doctor Sunshine chimed in:

"With one hand on the bottle, and the other on the throttle, singing," the rest of the birds came in, "I'm fresh out of beer!"

Everybody laughed. The good times were fun. Captain Whitey walked slowly. It was hot and humid. There was no rush back to camp. He stopped at a trash can and poked around. There was nothing of interest. The birds got bored of standing on his shoulders. Most of them flew down onto the mail cart. Finch disappeared under a piece of paper in the right-side pouch, and fell asleep. Bunker and Moiler and Beeper flew down onto the top of the cart and dug their heads into their chests and hit the sack. Detective Rabbi and Doctor Sunshine stayed behind. Detective Rabbi was on his left shoulder, Doctor Sunshine on his right. Captain Whitey could feel both of them about to disembark. They grabbed his shoulder skin with their claws and adjusted their weight, about to take flight. He stopped them. He said:

"Halt." They both shit on his respective shoulders. Then relaxed. Bobbed a little. Pecked at their chests. Rubbed the tops of their heads with their wings. Made a cooing noise. Then relaxed in earnest. Squatting, but not roosting. Captain Whitey waited as they did this. He needed their full attention. When he got it, he said, "I've been stupid. I know you both know this. I am wrong and I am foolish and I'm sorry. You're right. A parlay needs no politics, no love. Business is business. A dog barks in Nantucket, a whaler moans. I moan. You know what I mean?" Both Detective Rabbi and Doctor Sunshine bobbed. "What I mean is politics. It's now or never. We either parlay for glory, or give lub for lub's bounty. Smoke pipes, and watch the fire coal, kissing black things, getting black lips."

"Ack!" Doctor Sunshine took this as an affront. "Parlay is an essence. We will get there when we get there."

"Fuck that noise, throw another log on the fire!" Detective Rabbi was flapping his wings. "Why not?"

"Why not? What is glory without goals?"

"What are goals without understanding?"

"Who needs understanding?!"

"Who needs goals?!"

They were yelling at each other from each side of Captain Whitey's head. He became dizzy. He told them to stop. They didn't. He yelled:

"Stop it! I hate it when you fight!"

"Wasn't me, was Sunshine," Detective Rabbi said under his breath.

"Unh-uh, you started it." Doctor Sunshine's tone was aggressive.

"Wanna bet?" Detective Rabbi flew o ver a nd t ackled Doctor Sunshine off of Captain Whitey's shoulder. They fell to the ground wrestling. A cloud of dust appeared. Curses. "Lubber!" "Dock whore!" "I'll rip your dick off, you pickled cunt!" Just then Detective Rabbi bit Doctor Sunshine's crotch. "Yipe, yipe, yipe!" he screamed. He rolled away and suddenly there was a knife at the tip of his wing. "I'll cut you!" "Cut me in a dream, you better wake up and apologize." Detective Rabbi had a knife now too. They were circling each other. It was at this moment a cat pounced out of nowhere and grabbed Doctor Sunshine. Captain Whitey didn't think, he just acted. The kick to the cat's gut sent it flying twenty feet away. It landed with a thud. Doctor Sunshine fell out of its mouth. The cat skitted off without a sound. Captain Whitey ran over to Doctor Sunshine. The men came too, even Finch. Doctor Sunshine was lying in a pool of blood. His yellow feathers a strangely beautiful contrast to the glistening red. He was breathing quickly. His guts were strung out on the concrete. He was reaching out for something. His wing looked like he was trying to grab something. The tip curled. Captain Whitey scooped him up and held him in his hands. He said:

"Oh god, Sunshine, stay with me!" He was trying to put Doctor Sunshine's guts back into his insides.

"It got me, dog," Doctor Sunshine moaned in a whisper.

"That cur! Oh god, I am so sorry, Sunshine, stay with me." Tears were streaming down Captain Whitey's cheeks. He had to sit down. He made a circle with his legs. He held Doctor Sunshine in the middle. His men all jumped up, watching. Horror and shock played equal games on their faces. Tears dripped down the tips of their beaks. "Stay with me."

"Oh blackness, they're here for me. Not long now. It hurts, oh god!" Doctor Sunshine let out a groan.

"No! Don't leave me!" Captain Whitey was rubbing his thumb on Doctor Sunshine's head. It took all his effort to not just run away and pretend this wasn't happening.

"It's ok. Don't worry, don't worry. I'll see you soon. Promise me…," Doctor Sunshine trailed off. Captain Whitey lifted him to his ear. He said:

"What, promise you what?" His hands were shaking. He looked like he was about to roll dice.

"Parlay."

85

Doctor Sunshine died. He let out a gasp and shit on Captain Whitey's hand. Captain Whitey stood up. The birds flew to the mail cart. Captain Whitey walked over. Captain Whitey put the macerated body of Doctor Sunshine in the bottom of one of the pouches. He was so gentle he could have sewn spider webs. He put the flap down and pushed the mail cart forward. His men sat on the mail cart's spine. Not a word was spoken. Every movement had meaning, so they stood as still as they could.

When they got back to camp Captain Whitey found a big chunk of tree bark. He needed paper too. Strangely the money he had dumped out of the mail cart was lying in a pile where he had left it. He didn't think this was strange, but it was a strange thing. His men watched him do this in silence. He laid the money in a crosshatch on top of the tree bark. When he was done he went to the mail cart and took Doctor Sunshine's body out. It was already cold and jumping with insects. Captain Whitey put Doctor Sunshine's body on top of the money on top of the tree bark. He folded the wings over his chest and adjusted his head into a dignified position. In his mind Doctor Sunshine looked peaceful. In reality he looked like a gutted bird on top of a pile of money on top of a hunk of tree bark.

Captain Whitey took the thing that was his favorite friend down to the canal. He squatted down by the bank. His men flew over and landed beside him. He nodded at the water and said:

"I don't try to understand this life. It is what it is. But when a bird comes around of this caliber, it makes you think. I've never known one to peck with such gusto, coo with such abandon, roost like it's the only thing you will ever know, and parlay, well, his parlays were epic! This bird! He was a bird of abandon. Pure of heart. The most sincere bird I ever knew. Goodbye, Sunshine, may all your ports empty your pipes and leave you free of disease!"

Captain Whitey lit a match. The paper money caught easy. He lifted the pyre and put it on top of the canal water. It burned for a while. There was a film of oil on top of the water that caught fire. The fire spread quick. Soon the banks were on fire. Captain Whitey panicked. He went from being really sad to running for his life. He grabbed the mail cart and ran as fast as he could. Before he got to the street he tripped on a tree root. He fell down and knocked his head. Lights out.

86

The fire department came and put the fire out. They paid no attention to Whitey. He looked like a bum sleeping on the grass. He dreamed about flying with Doctor Sunshine. Holding the tip of his wing as they flew over the kingdom that would soon be theirs. Doctor Sunshine said:

"This is all ours, Cappy, all ours." He turned his head and smiled at Captain Whitey.

"So true." Captain Whitey bit his lip he was so happy.

Whitey woke up hungry and dehydrated next to the Gowanus Canal, splayed out on a comfortable patch of grass. He had no clue as to what had happened.

Special Thanks

Miette Gillette
Tina Satter
Michael Jung
Jack Warren
George Truman
Murphey Wilkins
Jonathan Butterick

About the Author

Joey Truman is a writer/performer/musician, in precisely that order. He has performed most notably with Norway-based Findlay//Sandsmark, The Collapsable Giraffe, and Um, a Brooklyn-based band. Previous titles with Whisk(e)y Tit include *Postal Child*, *Killing the Math*, and *KinderRinder*. His next title, *Cockroach Cooking: A Guide to Modern Poverty*, will be released by Whisk(e)y Tit in late 2018.

About the Publisher

Whisk(e)y Tit is committed to restoring degradation and degeneracy to the literary arts. We work with authors who are unwilling to sacrifice intellectual rigor, unrelenting playfulness, and visual beauty in our literary pursuits, often leading to texts that would otherwise be abandoned in today's largely homogenized literary landscape. In a world governed by idiocy, our commitment to these principles is an act of civil service and civil disobedience alike.